SEIZED

a novel by

Emma Tennant

OTHER FICTION

The Bad Sister

Wild Nights

Alice Fell

Queen of Stones

Woman, Beware Woman

Black Marina

Two Women of London:
The Strange Case of Ms Jekyll and Mrs Hyde

Faustine

Pemberley

The Ballad of Sylvia and Ted

Felony: A Private History of The Aspern Papers

The Harp Lesson

The French Dancer's Bastard

MEMOIRS

Strangers: A Family Romance

Girlitude

Burnt Diaries

SEIZED

a novel by

Emma Tennant

MAIA

Published in 2008 by
The Maia Press Limited
82 Forest Road
London E8 3BH
www.maiapress.com

ISBN 978 1 904559 31 3

A CIP catalogue record for this book is available
from the British Library

Printed and bound in Latvia by Dardedze Holography
on paper from sustainable managed forests

The Maia Press is supported by Arts Council England

1

I'm in the baggage reclaim section of Kerkyra International Airport – it's boiling hot and everyone's shouting at the same time – and through the glass I can see piles of luggage no one can be bothered to bring in because the carousel is broken.

I'll tell you why I'm here. Julie, that's my grandmother, didn't know what to do with me for the summer holidays because she's decided to marry someone I've only met twice and go and live up in Scotland. I'm to look out for a cab-driver called Tasso, who'll take me to the boat. You need a boat, Julie says, because there's no road to the house I'm going to stay in, the house where Cara, a hardly-ever-mentioned sister of Julie's, lives. All through the flight here I've been thinking: how will I ever get away? And then: tough, Aly, they won't let you spend the summer on your own in London so they send you off to a place where you're as good as locked up for the whole holidays until September.

Not for the first time in my life, I wonder what my mother would have done – would she have helped me or taken the side of Julie, who says when I come back I'll have to go and live in the North with her and the guy she'll have married by then. I'll never know what my mother would do, of course.

Tasso is the fat, bustling cab-driver. He has wispy white hair and when he sees the baggage beginning to move slowly round he goes mad with excitement, dancing and waving at me because he's already picked me out in the crowd. Maybe it's because I'm the only one on this charter flight of oldies who looks like a fifteen-year-old schoolgirl. And just how cool a thought is that?

But there's someone standing next to Tasso. Tall, maybe about sixteen or seventeen, with a mouth that looks as if it's never tried to smile. He's good-looking, in a kind of super-thin way – but he looks cross, like the black labrador my friend Liberty brought back from Battersea Dogs' Home. It sulked and growled and one day it just wasn't there any more. But there's no more time for first impressions – and mine are usually wrong anyway – because Tasso is pulling me through the crowd and the luggage is coming in and thudding down on the frayed rubber and I'm pulling my bag (one of the first and that's a first) and humping it on to a trolley the young guy with Tasso has found somewhere. I don't know his name until we're out in front of the notice saying ARRIVALS. Tasso goes off to get his cab and we stand staring at each other. 'Stefanos,' says this person I'm supposed to spend the entire summer with, in a roadless house. And I say I'm Aly, but he looks as if the name doesn't mean anything to him and he doesn't want me to say it again.

I suppose it's the heat and the very special smell of Greece that greets you when you first arrive there. A sort of mixture of honey and herbs that don't smell so strong when Julie brings them back from the market in North End Road, rosemary and thyme. Thrown in with it all there's a strong whiff of petrol, as well as dust from the roadworks and the house building all round the airport – but the wild mountain smell wins every time. And I think for one moment before the big coaches rev up and the package people jostle out on to the pavement: maybe I'll run away and explore those mountains. Julie and this sister of hers can hunt for me but I'll have disappeared. You'll have gathered from this that a future life in Dundee with a newly-wed granny is not my idea of bliss.

Tasso's cab is just as bumpy and springs-gone as you might expect if you'd seen the holiday videos other people at school showed when they were still too young to know better. There's a driver just like Tasso with an 'I'm trying to be friendly but I want a big tip' smile. (OK, I'm cynical about strangers who talk to you as if they've known you all your life.) And often there's an old wreck of a taxi in the picture too. Parents usually give an affectionate laugh at this bit, I find it all sickening.

The island of Kerkyra, as the guide-books tell you, is long and thin and narrow. What they don't say is how long it takes to get out of the town – if that's what all those squashed-tomato-coloured houses and teetering high-rise blocks belong to. No sign of all the Venetian houses etc. puffed by the guide, just nasty suburbs.

OK, I'm sitting in the back of the cab on a scorching and sagging black plastic seat and Stefanos is in front with Tasso, and I must have dozed off. The tang of Tasso's and Stefanos's Greek cigarettes and the sound of a mobile phone ringing and ringing (whose is it? why don't they answer?) make me open my eyes and pull forward so I can look out. A wasp blows in the open window and lands on Stefanos's neck. He kills it – whack! – before it can sting him, and he flicks it out on to the road. Then Tasso is listening on his phone and he turns to Stefanos and says something that sounds like *askimos kairos*. Stefanos just shrugs. They look like this, as if it's a row they've had several times and neither wins.

This is where I have to say all the things people are supposed to say when they see some foreign place or another for the first time – but I just have to, so here goes. The sad, DIY-looking houses and run-down apartment blocks had all disappeared and we were in open country. There's a huge plain, all empty and bare and criss-crossed by streams and little bridges and at the edges of the plain are gigantic olive trees. Julie had gone on about the four-hundred-year-old olives planted by the Venetians on the island and how lovely they were, and I'd said, Why don't you ever go there then, Gran? But she just looked sad as she always does when the subject comes up. And rising above the olive forests are the mountains, like a burnt-out volcano making a great ring round the plain. The sun is low in the sky and they kind of smoulder, so high it is impossible to imagine running along and jumping from peak to peak – although of course I did. If this was where the gods came from, I could believe the myths you have crammed into you from cartoons onwards. Why wouldn't the gods want to live in a place like this?

I only realised the row between Tasso and Stefanos was still going on – although silently – when the old taxi reached the end of the plain and turned left with a loud squeal into a dusty road leading downwards and very steep.

What I saw now made me just want to go faster and jump right in – to the blue blue sea – and dive and swim until a wave washed me on to the beach, just visible hundreds of feet below. I must have shouted out something, because Tasso jammed on the brakes and the car, as if it couldn't believe this was really happening, finally came to a halt in a cloud of white dust. There were pine trees now at the side of the road and the sea could only be glimpsed through the dark branches. A strong resin smell came in with the heat. 'I stop here,' Tasso said in English, to let us know he meant business I supposed, because Stefanos just scowled even more and swung out of the cab on to the unmade road. I got out of the car, pulling my bag behind me. I could hear the sea now, as it pounded and crashed below. 'Bora Maestro,' Tasso said. (I didn't know what he meant, but later I discovered it was the north wind which makes the sea too rough for any but the biggest boats.) I stood watching as he reversed into a precipitous hole by the side of the road. The car paused, shuddered, and finally turned its nose upward – then the dust came into my eyes and lungs and I ran downhill.

2

I'm down in a bay where a lot of boats are moored up against each other, but there's no sign of anyone in them. I'm looking for Stefanos and I'm thinking he looks like the kind of guy who would do this – run off and leave a stupid English girl to fend for herself in a country where she can't speak the language and God I don't even know the address of the house where Julie's sister lives.

I can understand why Tasso the taxi-driver refused to come down the last stretch of road before you get to the bay. Big waves are splashing across it from the rocks and they're timing themselves so a car wouldn't have a chance if a Greek variation of a tsunami came up just under the cliff. Already, smashed oars and bits of driftwood are bobbing about on petrolly water and the boats are groaning as they nudge each other by a broken-looking jetty. There isn't even a café in sight, so I can't ring the number Julie gave me. And I did bring my mobile although it would cost so much to ring home on it, but Julie would get really annoyed. (I smuggled it into my bag and she searched but never found it.) Julie teaches dancing and aerobics and she's always short of money – she'll re-use teabags by drying them out on the radiator. The thought of a mobile phone bill from Greece would be enough to keep her quiet and miserable-looking for at least a week.

Stefanos is walking along the rotting pier and he holds a coil of rope that seems to be attached to a kind of rowing-boat with an engine, larger than the boats on the Serpentine in Hyde Park but not much. I go up to him and suddenly start to feel sick – are we supposed to go out on the open sea in that, I'm asking myself? And then I'm asking him, but he just says nothing and doesn't smile either, as usual. Not that there's much to smile about, I agree. I don't see any sign of a lifejacket in the boat either – and I never thought I'd think fussy things like that. So I jump down, nearly twisting my ankle, and I'm on a narrow ledge that's the only seating in the boat, and Stefanos is yanking at the engine to start it up. We go backwards too fast, and he slows us down before we run right into a moving yacht, and then we make a full circle and go in leaps and jumps out to the opening to the bay. A hill with a lighthouse on it looms up in front of us and then we've left it behind and, wow, there's nothing ahead of us except this bright, bright blue with sprays of white foam on the crest of each wave. I take a long, deep breath and the salt and the diesel from the engine and smoke from Stefanos's big fat

Greek cigarette all go right down inside me so I'm giddy but I don't care.

The house is visible on the far side of a wide bay, which has rocks and slopes with trees on both sides coming down into deep water. It stands above a long white beach – it could be sand or shingle, you can't tell at this distance, and just under the house is a valley with huge bushes covered in pink and white flowers and a whole lot of olive trees swaying silver and green in this strong wind that must be a Bora Maestro. The house is white with blue window-frames and there are swallows flying in and out of the roof and a terrace where they skim over the tops of the trees before flying out to sea.

It is the most beautiful place I have ever seen in my life. And I say to myself – but the wind takes my words and forces them back down my throat again – why didn't Julie ever tell me it was like this?

—

Then the sea got rough, I mean really rough, so the white foam on the waves disappeared and walls of water that were a much grimmer colour than the Med blue we'd been in started going at the boat from all sides. One minute we were high up, perched – me on the narrow ledge and holding on to the place where an oar was meant to go (but no sign of an oar anywhere) and Stefanos opposite keeping a tight grip on the tiller. Every time a trick mountain wave tried to swamp us, he swung the piece of wood around, showing we could play our own tricks if we wanted to. One minute, as I say, we were high, high and it looked as if we'd fly on to the long strip of beach with no trouble. The next, we were down under and so low it seemed we'd never be able to heave ourselves up. At those times I was frightened – I've never been a good swimmer. Waiting for the times when the house and the beach came nearer was as close as I've ever got to thinking I was about to die.

I can't say when it was clear the sea had changed sides and actually wanted us to arrive on dry land. It was about the time it became possible to see three figures standing up to their knees in water and waving at us as if nothing extraordinary was happening. It was when I saw the little stone jetty, perhaps, that sticks out just by the cliff at the end of the beach. There's a cave like a black hole all the way up it. But it still seemed about as unlikely that we'd get to the jetty while these monster waves were pushing us around as – well, as anything I've ever prayed for. And now I prayed we wouldn't go straight into the black hole. I saw us sailing on in a dark cavern we'd never find our way out of, propelled by a huge wall of water.

But we glided up to the jetty as if the sea wasn't rough at all and Stefanos jumped out and ran along the small cement pier that was submerged half the time and visible the other half, so you had to judge carefully when you stepped – or jumped – out of the boat. The sea was dark and quite deep here and I thought, God, Aly, you have got to get this right or you'll be soaked to the skin and on top of that your bag will go down with you. Where's Stefanos, how did he run along the jetty and jump the surging lake between the end of the pier and the shingle beach? And I suppose I'm telling you this because that was when I first realised there was something about Stefanos that no one would ever be able to pin down.

Three sets of hands reach out to me. The first pair belong to a boy (about twelve, very dark like Stefanos, must be his younger brother) who pulls me along the jetty and hoists my bag on to his shoulder with a grin that makes me like him. Perhaps because Stefanos never smiles, I don't know. The next hands are those of a boy who can't be more than eight years old – and who, clearly, cannot swim as he keeps falling down in the surf and having to be pulled out by his sister.

At least, that's what I imagine she is. A small, slightly built girl – fair-haired, unlike the others, and with grey eyes that are smarting from salt water because she's trying to wipe them when she's not signalling to the eldest to throw my bag on to the pebbles before any more spray goes all over it. Then I'm on the beach – and, yes, I misjudged and landed smack in the big sea puddle lying in wait at the end of the jetty. But somehow it doesn't matter because the girl is shouting over the crash of the waves that she is Vasso and the two boys are Mario and Michaelis and she tugs me by the hand. So we set off together across the beach and we don't turn back once to look at the sea.

We went up flights of stone steps to the terrace. You can't see the steps from the beach because bushes and shrubs and what look like palm trees are growing so thick all the way up to the house that you think there's no way up at all. And the steps are laid with pebbles which hurt the soles of your feet and make going up there even more difficult than you could ever have thought. Maybe whoever constructed all this wanted to suggest a pilgrimage of some kind – and by the time I've doubled back on to another flight of steps and passed the lower part of the house – it looks a bit like a prison, this lower part, thick yellow stone and no windows, just a chunky big door – I'm having to remind myself that the present owner probably laid the pebbles, and she's Julie's sister, my great-aunt Cara. It's hard to believe because obviously the whole place is so unlike Julie, with her small house near the North End Road and the tiny garden she tries to keep neat but just doesn't have the energy for, these days. And I wonder, did Julie ever come here and if she did, didn't she ask if she could come back again and again? Because, by the time I'm up the last flight and on the terrace, I've decided it's the only place in the world I ever want to be.

Now I see the boys have run off down the terrace and only Vasso is left, standing ahead of me under the tiled roof where the swallows fly in and out. The sun is so strong in my eyes I can only just pick out a long glass door leading in to the house from this place I think is called a verandah, and I stumble against a tall pot that has a very bright blue flower in it, as I follow Vasso to the door. 'Alissa' – that's Vasso trying out my name – and I'm right behind her and walking into a long, vaulted room where all the white curtains are drawn and, as far as I can see, still blinded by the change from sun to darkness, a woman is lying back on one of the long white sofas, reading a book. 'Kiria,' Vasso says, and the woman looks up and across the back of the sofa at us. She's pulled her glasses up on to her head, her hair is brownish fair, and the first thing I notice is her arms are very brown, so brown it looks like she's been out in the sun all her life and never gone pale like girls at school who go for a holiday in the Med and get paler and paler as term goes on. She swings her legs off the sofa and they're thin and brown too. She's part of the place, I remember thinking, and although she must be old if she's Julie's sister, she looks as if age has forgotten her altogether.

It's hard to describe Cara and I'm not going to try now because the pace of things – which had slowed down so much when Vasso and I first went in to that long, dark room that you could hear the minutes ticking on a clock (another surprise: a cheap clock on the chest of drawers that looks as if it doesn't belong here at all) – the pace suddenly picked up and a whole lot of things happened at once.

The first thing was the bony cheek that came down to meet mine, and a feathery kiss which came with it. 'You are here. I am Cara,' came next. 'I'm surprised you were able to get over' – and she waved vaguely at a pair of white curtains drawn across a vast window. So I imagine she must think I know my way around here already and am aware these curtains are hiding the sea. 'Vasso, ask Sofia to come and meet Alice' – and then, to me, 'You're a painter like I am? This is a good place for painting, you know, Alice! Look at mine! Look around you. Did you bring paints?'

I suppose this is the only way to describe my one short meeting with the woman Julie told me would keep an eye on me for the next six weeks. Her paintings, hard, dry paint in searing blues and strong browns and yellows, were strangely like Cara: you admired them but you certainly didn't want to get any nearer. She laughed – and if it's possible to laugh with a foreign accent, that's what she did. And she went round, pausing under the high, vaulted ceiling at each of her pictures, spelling out the names of the houses and villages and mountains and plains she'd painted, and stopping always longest at the pictures of the sea. 'I have a show in Athens,' she said. And just as she spoke, staring up at the ceiling as if she were going to meditate or pray or something, the next thing happened – which was Stefanos came in and didn't stop at the door but went right up to her and started speaking in Greek. 'Nai,' Cara goes, before he can even finish his sentence, and he's out of the long room again at double speed. And to me, 'He wants to go out in the big caique. You'll see it in one of my paintings – on the stairs out there, he goes out fishing in the big caique. Go and look at the painting, Alice. You'll see others of the island of Mathraki higher up.'

So that was how I found myself half-way up a staircase in the centre of the house staring at a Greek fishing boat in a harbour, and then on a landing with bookcases crammed with dusty books and open doors where you could see the blue glint of the sea in the windows of the rooms they led into. And although I didn't really think clearly then that it was strange I hadn't been asked how my journey was or told where I would sleep, I really didn't mind at all.

3

In the event it was easy to find my room because someone had brought my bag up from downstairs and I knew it must be Vasso because she was the only person to be friendly to me as if she meant it (you can't count Cara – I can tell she's one of those people who's best friends mainly with herself). The room is small and right at the end of the corridor off the landing, and what with the tall wood cupboard and a pretty old-looking basin with brown marks inside and misty colour taps, you might say it was nothing to write home about. Not that I'm going to write to Julie because she's put the London house up for sale and gone flat-hunting in Scotland with this man she's going to marry. She wants the company, I suppose. And I can just imagine her giving one of her funny looks when she sees my room. No room to swing a cat here, she'd say. Where are you going to do your course work for next term? But then Julie thinks with her body – if she can kick her legs out and twirl round like she does in her exercise classes, then the space she's in is just right. In here, it's so tight and there's just an inch or two of floor before you have to fall on to the bed.

Vasso has put my bag in the big cupboard (there's nowhere else for it) and she goes to open the shutters and then everything changes again. She has an odd way of being near just when you think of her and I don't know if she followed me down the corridor or was waiting here for me all along.

'The sea,' Vasso says. 'Thalassa.' And I look out of the window over a vine that grows on a metal frame just below and has dark red grapes and a few wasps that are attacking them. Then there's another sound, it's a kind of throbbing as if the whole valley and the hill opposite the house going down to the cliff with the big black hole just above the beach is following an endless rhythm that seems to go with the heat and the sun, which is lower in the sky. I look at the sea, calm now and a bright blue, that's like the crayon drawings of the sea pinned up on the board in the primary school where Julie gives classes once a week. The beat of the crickets – if that's what they are – and the sheer size of the view make the room seem huge now, instead of tiny, and Vasso must know I feel that because she laughs when I step back from the window and show I'm a bit giddy with it all by falling down on the bed.

Vasso is clever and she can speak English, too, when she feels like it. She says, 'I have this to give you.' And she hands me an envelope with my name on it, a cheap, almost transparent envelope. For some reason I don't want to open it at once – or maybe I don't want Vasso to see I'm having difficulty reading. (It's why I have special tuition, it's called dyslexia and it's better than it was when I was nine or ten, when every word came out backwards and there was an impatient teacher, who left before she could make people like me feel we didn't have a chance and give up altogether.)

So I stuff the letter in my pocket and I ask Vasso to show me more of this place that she says is called Villa Marilli, because it was Cara's grandmother's name. Then she says am I hot, why don't we go down to the sea, and then she's gone and I'm pulling my swimming costume out of my bag and this time I run after her down the pebbled steps without feeling the sharp bits underfoot and Vasso runs ahead with the two boys Michaelis and Mario, who've seen us and swooped down a flight of steps from a shabby-looking little house just behind the white villa on its terrace overlooking the sea.

And then I'm in the sea. The water is so clear you can see little fish swimming under you and rocks and pebbles on the sea-bed that look much bigger than they really are if you dive down and pick one up. It's like being in a giant magnifying glass and the sun going down over the horizon makes a path you're tempted to swim along, all the way to Italy. 'I like it here,' I say to Vasso, as she pulls away from the youngest, Michaelis, and he and his brother start up a splashing war in the shallows. And Vasso calls out that this is her mother coming down the steps. That's when I find out that the kids' mum is Sofia – and Matthias their father is following her down to the beach where the bright orange nets are laid out. Then the sun vanishes under the line of sea in the far distance and it's suddenly half-light and half-dark, with the crickets getting louder, and I don't want to leave the sea because it's exactly the same temperature as my blood.

Sofia is a plump woman in a dress with a big flower pattern and she turns and looks at me as I come out of the sea. The small boat I came over in – years ago, OK, earlier today – is pulled right up to the entrance to the black hole and she's disentangling the nets with her husband. They place their nets in the boat and by the time I've made my second arrival at Marilli Bay – as Vasso says it's called by locals and tourists who come to swim in the clear water here – Matthias and Sofia have finished their work and have begun the trudge across the beach to the steps and (presumably) their own cottage hidden by the trees. They haven't waved or said hello to me – but I know from Susan, the girl in my year who goes to Greece every summer, that you have to be the first to exchange greetings – otherwise you're just a stranger people ignore. And I wish I'd remembered that before it was too late.

—

By the time I'd gone upstairs and pulled the clothes out of my bag, it was seriously night-time and now I know when the sun goes down you only have about twenty minutes before the night whirrers are out and the crickets have gone quiet. They were flying into my room, great black moths and a bat which got tangled up in the curtain. (But I don't mind bats since I went on summer camp and found a whole colony in a ruined abbey we were taken to see. They were harmless really and the girls who screamed looked stupid.)

I've found a bathroom which must be Cara's. I don't think there's another, but this is an old house so why would there be? And at first I felt too frightened to go in but there was no one up on the first floor and after I'd gone to the bathroom I even peeped into Cara's bedroom and stood there a while to feel what she really likes about the place.

Well, I'll tell you, it's the sea that Cara really loves, as if the pictures she paints didn't give that away already. There are four windows in the big bedroom off the landing and they all look out at the sea – invisible now, of course, in this black night that's lit only with low lights on the terrace and – a film-star touch, this – spotlighting on the black hole so it looks like a cave in a theatrical set. But you can hear the sea very clearly from this room. By the sound of it, it's getting up again and there's a muffled crashing from the pebble beach which makes me glad I'm not in a boat trying to come in.

In spite of this, what I really felt was a creepy silence and it took me a little time before I realised the silence meant there was no one actually in the house, not downstairs or up. I'd heard Sofia earlier (I imagine it was Sofia talking fast in Greek from behind the kitchen door that leads off the hall) and I thought I'd heard Vasso coming along the corridor to my room. I'd got used to her kindness already and I suppose I expected her to tell me what I should do next. Was I to go into the long, vaulted room and talk to Cara? Were we going to have dinner together outside, under the roof where the swallows must be asleep by now? Was I to help with the meal or what? I knew somehow that Vasso and her brothers wouldn't eat with Cara – but where had they gone and was I welcome to go along to their house in the trees? – which, I may say, I knew I'd far rather do than be with my great aunt all alone and searching for something interesting to say.

No answer came. The walls of Cara's room, just about the only part of the house not hung with her paintings, were plain white and I stood staring at them as if the solution might appear there. I gazed at her bedside table, where china plates covered in shells and blue and green stones from the sea were jumbled up with pill bottles. I gazed across the width of the room at her dressing-table and saw a drawer pulled out, a dried-up bottle of ink in it and what looked like those bundles of old papers you see on TV documentaries when they try to teach you about history. On the table itself, there was a flaky tray decorated with a seascape and there were a few old lipsticks on it but otherwise nothing at all.

And I thought, I knew, that Cara wasn't only not in the house – she wasn't here at all. She'd left a kind of imprint of herself – but she had gone.

—

Supper was outside the back door that goes into the kitchen from the bit of terrace you arrive at, I imagine, if you don't have the honour of Stefanos bringing you over by boat and you walk down a path as far as the steps. A long table was set up under a very bright light and everyone was eating already – even Vasso, who gave a friendly wave but didn't do anything more. So I pulled out a chair with a wonky leg that no one else had wanted to sit on, and I tried to remember to say 'Herete,' which Susan at school said was hi or something like it. As I did this I looked round the table and there was little Michaelis with his sly look I'd noticed earlier – sly but bitter and sad, too, as if he knew no one could find the time for him.

There was Mario sitting next to his father Matthias at the end of the table by the corner of the house. There was Vasso right across from me. And at the foot of the table, the only vacant place for my wonky chair to go, sprawled over his half-full plate, was Stefanos. A fag smoulders on a metal saucer, and a bottle of red wine is on the table in front of him. He pours more into his glass. Sofia, with Vasso next to her, is ladling food on to a plate and she says, 'Pastizzia,' and looks at me and laughs.

So I begin to understand that none of the family seems pleased to see me here at all.

—

There's something weird about being in a house alone and knowing nobody cares if you're stuck there forever or you run away. Downstairs there's a tiny room off the kitchen with two single beds at right angles and a black-and-white medium-sized TV – I looked in when I'd eaten (a silent meal, punctuated by belches from Matthias) – and after I'd had this pastizzia, a kind of tepid macaroni with mince, but I was hungry, I got up and left the table and Mario darted past me and into the TV room. I stood staring at him a moment – could I ask him if Cara had gone for good? Was she coming back tonight? But Mario already had a football match on at full pitch and I saw Sofia coming through with her heavy walk from outdoors so I bolted upstairs. Why all this tension? Surely Vasso will come and say goodnight and answer my questions? But, as you can tell, she didn't, and here I am completely alone in the Villa Marilli, because I heard the back door slam miles below and worst of all a noise horribly like a big rusty key turning in the lock.

Before you say blame this on an over-active gothic imagination or something of the sort, I'd like to remind you that I've been self-sufficient for a long time now. Julie was usually doing one class or another when I got home after school. I was a latch-key kid (well, some of the time) and I did shopping at Tesco, so I know their heat-up macaroni is much more tasty than Sofia's pastizzia and how to get the raspberries cheap if they're just past their sell-by date. I don't mind being alone. I even like it when there's a film I want to watch on TV (Julie's made us into the only people we're likely to meet who don't actually own a DVD player). Of course I like phoning my friends . . .

Now here comes the bad news. My mobile phone is in my bag, and as I'm sitting on my bed (it may be black night outside but PLEASE it's only 9.30 p.m. and I absolutely refuse to give up and actually get under the covers) I pull it out and think I'll give Liberty just one quick call and tell her all the strange things about this place. And, you guessed it, there is no signal and I throw the phone back into the bag, not very difficult in a room this size and this time I really do feel I might cry. When you think of it, of course, Cara would live in a place where there's no mast and if there was the threat of one going up on her land I can just see her stopping it.

Cut to the fact I'd left the shutters open earlier and night insects are rushing in, attracted by the bedside lamp, and you have all the ingredients for a horror story. I'm not going to write one, though, even if Mary Shelley was only eighteen when she wrote *Franken-*

stein in a spooky villa on some lake or other, not so unlike here I expect.

So I go ahead in the way I would if I hadn't been abandoned in a house where the family who look after the absent owner are not, repeat not, thrilled to have me here. Maybe they wanted a holiday. If you live in a paradise like Marilli Bay, where DO you go for a holiday? West London on a rainy day?

Anyway, I decided to sleep in my clothes *for safety's sake*, and I washed in the old basin with the steamed-up taps because I somehow didn't feel like going out in the corridor and into Cara's bathroom, that's how spooked I was. But I felt better when I'd brushed my teeth and then I went to lie down under the duvet cover and then I decided I wanted a pee so I had to go out in the corridor and into Cara's bathroom after all. Her pictures were all over the walls and as I went into her bathroom I saw the paintings of the sea, stiff and white-capped like it had been earlier when Stefanos brought me over in the little boat.

And I turned off the bedside lamp (brave) but left on the corridor lights (sensible in my view – suppose Cara came back and couldn't find the way to her room?)

But I knew somehow that Cara wasn't coming back. Not tonight anyway. I was alone. And after I'd counted the euros in my head that must be in my bag along with my passport I thought about how I would get out of Marilli Bay when there is no road down to the house and how on earth I would find a taxi to take me to the airport when my phone wasn't working and the house phone (I saw one in the hall) was probably connected to Sofia's cottage. They'd make every effort to get me back, whether they liked me or not. They work for Cara, after all.

Then I thought about my mother. I only do that if I feel really lonely or sad. I wonder if she ever came here – with Julie perhaps? – and what happened before Julie and Cara had The Big Row they must have had all those years ago.

No ideas come. Just thinking of her always makes me feel better, though, if all I can remember of her is her very cool hands when I was sick and she laid them on my forehead to see if I had a temperature. And even that memory, as I know, might be invented.

I fell asleep.

—

I was woken by a bright light shining in on me and I knew it wasn't daytime because the little plastic alarm clock Julie made me bring out here said in green letters on a black background that it was 1 a.m.

The moon is so bright – there'd been no sign of it in the evening but now it's as round as a gold coin up in the sky, and it's throwing a strange white light on the olive trees below my window and on the beach which looks like a long scroll of paper no one would ever dare write on, it's so perfectly ghostly and smooth.

The sea is lapping up the moon's rays, it's gone a dark silver colour and the water is making a sound as if an army of prisoners were dragging their chains, when it sucks in and pushes out on the shore. There's a lonely feeling, as if this bay knew itself best long before this house was built here and there were just the olives nodding in the wind on their way down to the beach and the cave open and black on the side of the cliff.

I leant right out of the window above Cara's grapes and stared at the big boat as it rocked in deep water, moored about sixty or seventy feet out to sea.

It was the boat, the same one as Cara's painting on the stairs and it had the same name, *Faleina,* that she had written in neat lettering on the prow of the boat in her picture. A Greek deep-sea fishing-boat Julie says is called a caique, it looked unsinkable, with its wide wooden rail and a mast as thick as a big tree.

I thought of Stefanos and how he'd asked Cara if he could go out in the caique and then I thought of him at supper and how he'd got up from the table suddenly as if he knew this was the time for something, but you couldn't tell what. Why had it taken this long for him to bring the boat round to Marilli Bay? Where did the caique usually live, if not here? But I could see there was no natural harbour by this beach, and my own arrival had shown just how much damage the sea could do to a boat left here in a storm.

He must have waited – and it was true the wind had dropped and the olive trees in the grove stood almost still.

But something else didn't. The sound of marching feet grew loud in the grove and muffled voices rose as far as the window where I strained for a view in light so pale it was only another form of darkness.

I half-expected Stefanos's family – his father Matthias or even little Michaelis – to run from their cottage out on to the terrace at the sound of this column of people as they tramped down under the trees to the beach. But no one made a sound. Only when the small boat was dragged down over timber poles to the edge of the sea did the rasp of feet on shingle become audible at this height above the valley. Still none of the line of people – and there were small children among them, you could see their shadows in the moonlight, half the size of the others as they waited to embark – spoke or shouted or cried.

The small boat, with Stefanos revving up the engine each time it left shallow water so it wouldn't go on the rocks by the cave, made four trips to the big caique altogether. There may have been six on each trip squashed on the narrow ledge in the back and up on the bows, so about two dozen people were about to be taken somewhere by the *Faleina*.

Where or why it was impossible to say.

4

I don't know how long I stood at the window looking out when there was nothing left to see. When black clouds came across the sky and the moon started jigging over the mountains, it must have been, because I know my room looked tiny all over again without the moonlight flooding in and the olives nodding their heads, so near they could have been on the terrace and not right down in the grove. I turned on the bedside lamp (I'm not such a fool that I'd leave a light burning with all those night insects just waiting to be asked in) and I got in to the narrow bed that's only a couple of feet from the smelly old basin and I waited to go to sleep.

Nothing happened, of course. I kept seeing Stefanos at the oars of the little boat, bent over with the strain of rowing all those people to the big caique, the *Faleina*. Then I saw the column of marchers coming down to the beach under the trees. After that, I strained to remember whether Stefanos had actually said anything at supper last night that would help explain the night-time flight from Marilli Bay – and again, there were no clues at all. Once I heard the engines of a boat as it made its way across the bay, but I was too sleepy by then to get up and lean out of the window. I knew, somehow, that the growl of engines I heard didn't belong to the caique – it had gone and Stefanos with it. And I think, God, I'd be better off if I'd run down and joined all those unknown escapees – if that's what they were – than I'm going to be if I stay here.

I must have slept at last, because the next time I lifted my head it was broad daylight and I could feel my eyes hurting from the bright blue of the sea and a sun that came in straight at me – as if I had to learn somehow that I was in a foreign country and you have to close the shutters or you get boiled. Thinking about what I'd have missed if I *had* closed them though makes me decide I'm going to get up and go and find Vasso. I want to know what's going on here – and I almost make myself laugh: the voice I'm imagining saying that is more like our head teacher's than my own. Because who says I'll ever find out what scam Sofia's and Matthias's family are running?

The tall cupboard in my room produces the next surprise. It's when I rummage in my bag with all my stuff in it, on the floor of the cupboard, and I suppose I never noticed before what was actually hanging up there. Jackets – a man's jackets, and trousers on those old-fashioned press things I once saw when I was taken away for a country weekend in a posh place I think was Hampshire. (Julie hated the place and we left before lunch on Sunday.) On shelves by the side of the hanging space are shirts and pullovers.

I'm deciding these clothes look English but kind of made-ages-ago and I'm pulling my bag on to the bed when something falls out of the pocket of the jeans I was wearing last night before I put on a skirt in case I had to have dinner with my great-aunt Cara (well, it's not something I'd normally do, but Julie insisted I bring an outfit for when I needed to look respectable, as she rather cringingly put it).

What had fallen out was the envelope Vasso had given me when she first showed me this room. Through the thin paper I can see a card, and as I'm on my own I rip open the envelope and pull the card out. The first thing I see is a picture, and as I'm still feeling a bit weird after standing looking out at the *Faleina* for half of last night, it takes me a bit of time to realise the picture *is* actually of the caique Stefanos went off in with all those people. It's the picture on the stairs.

When I turn it over – and this makes me feel weirder still – there's an invitation lay-out and Cara, for it must be Cara, has scrawled my name, Alice, along the top and a couple of XXs, as if we'd known and loved each other for centuries, instead of just meeting for a few minutes last night.

It's not that that's making me walk the two feet to

the basin with the chipped mirror over it, however, and stare at my face as if I'd never seen it before. It's because for one terrifying, shattering second I really don't know who I am.

Before I go into a kind of apologetic explanation of what it's like to have been teased at primary school for writing my name ECILA and bullied – there's no other word for it – by the special needs teacher who made me stay with the same Janet and John for what seemed like ten years, I'll tell you here and now that I don't believe in all that Hallowe'en twaddle or OMEN etc, even if Liberty and her lot went through a really heavy haunted period about two years ago. I have what Julie will go on calling a disability, and I suppose it got to annoy me because she had a hard time leaving me notes about what I should heat up from the freezer when I got home from school. It made me depressed, seeing SHEPHERD'S PIE written in big letters, as if that would help. And the real reason I was depressed was because it made me feel I couldn't move or go anywhere without my gran spelling and printing it first.

Now, with Julie the control freak deciding my every move as usual, I find myself in a house on a bay in Greece and I'm wishing, wishing my phone wasn't cut off because it makes me think I'm in a house on a bay in the Middle Ages and it's not a feeling I like at all.

I'll try to tell Libs what happened. Libs, I say to the mirror with my face on it – Libs, it's the weirdest thing . . .

The door of the room opens, rather shyly and slowly, and Vasso's head appears round it, surprisingly low down, because it's hard to remember just how small Vasso is for her age (she told me she was thirteen, a year older than Mario and half his height).

Vasso is smiling. She says, 'Come fishing,' and for a moment I think she's telling me the *Faleina* is back from its expedition and Stefanos is going to take us all out where it's really deep. But Vasso is pointing out of my window at the rocks by the black hole in the cliff and she says 'octopodi' and then a word like 'barbouni' and she comes up to me and takes me by the hand as if she hadn't been sort of cut off and unfriendly the night before.

The rocks are hard to climb on, I think that's what she's saying, and she shakes her head when I pick up my swimming costume from the towel rail at the side of the basin. 'Ela,' she says, 'Come!'

And that's how I nearly forgot to say what the funny thing was that just happened before Vasso came in. Now I come to think of it, there *must be some mistake* and I was just tired and worked up after watching Stefanos's army embark on the caique and sail away.

It was a trick of the eyesight, that's all. But when I peeped again at the card Cara had left for me, it happened all over again.

The card was like this:

You are invited for a coffee
on Thursday afternoon at 6.00
Cara

in what must be Greek because I didn't know the letters at all.

But the strange part I was going to tell you about is that I could read it perfectly. I could understand it, too – Cara was inviting me for a coffee at the gallery where her pictures were on show. The name was printed below, the Nausicaa in Syndagma Square.

I've never written or spoken a word of Greek in my life.

But there was no time to think about that. Vasso was running and I went after her down the stairs and into the hall and out into the morning light.

—

As soon as I was out on the terrace by the great fig tree that starts one storey down by the side of the *stoa* (as Vasso says the lower part of the villa is called) and grows so high it pokes its huge leaves and purple fruit right over the edge of the balustrade, I forgot all the strange things I'd seen from the window of my little room last night.

I took a fig and bit into the red and gold veins that opened in its warm flesh. In the kitchen, behind the window's mosquito netting, I could hear Sofia running a tap and shouting something – but I didn't care whether I understood her or not.

I saw the sea so blue and flat it was impossible to

believe that it could froth up and turn hard and murderous, like in Cara's picture on the stairs where the thickness of the paint shows Marilli Bay as real and frightening as I'd known it when Stefanos brought me over, a long day and night-time ago.

I'm happy, I suppose, because the Matthias family are friendly again – Mario has run along from the cottage with a pair of orange flippers, Sofia actually smiled at me (they seem a bit short on smiles, this family) and young Michaelis has lost the resentful (if that's the right word) look he gives anyone who speaks to him at all.

There's a new addition to the place now, too. A dog, a big brown-and-white dog with a mournful face rather like Matthias's (I'll tell you about Matthias later) and he's here on the terrace with me because I heard him whining and barking in a shed at the back of the house and Vasso let him out. He's Stefanos's dog, she said – and when I asked why he wasn't taken out on the caique and Vasso stared at me as if I was a ten-year-old, I wished I'd kept my mouth shut.

The dog is called Oxo – at least that's what I thought, until I realised it just doesn't have a name at all and Oxo means Go Away, which is all he seems to have said to him in his life because he wags his tail when you say it and doesn't go anywhere. Oxo is my friend now – I know it's soppy but I've always wanted a dog, and a rabbit was as far pet-wise as Julie would go. It lived in a cage in the garden and one day she took it away and let it loose in the park – I know she did, and it took me a long time to forgive her for that.

At last we're all ready and we go down the steps into the grove and the slab of blue that is the sea is at the end of the trees. It's absolutely still, so it's hard to believe the olives can dance about when the wind gets up without losing their precious black harvest, if you think of all the tossing and straining they do, and it's true, today, there are nets down on the rough, baked-looking terraces where they grow, and we have to walk carefully unless we crush the tiny fruit underfoot. It's as if there might be an end to the summer coming – although there can't be for ages, yet.

It's hard to describe what a free feeling is like if you've probably never had one – not for longer than an hour or two, anyway. It's like something lifting off your shoulders and your head becomes very clear at the same time – you're free to go anywhere you like and you can see all the choices open out in front of you, with plenty of time to make up your mind.

Something like that, anyway. And it got better and better and this is how and why.

We climbed the rocks that were just like knives they were so sharp under the espadrilles Julie packed (and didn't put in my trainers because, she said, it would be too hot). Little Michaelis jabbed himself and almost cried – but then he must have felt happy, too, because he stopped almost at once.

We were right up the inside of the cave and we came out on to a narrow path that wound along the coast as far as the eye could see. You could double back and follow the path down to the grove that way, except it was more fun to scramble out of the hole at the top of the cave, like a sweep coming back out of a chimney.

All the time I'd been in the cave, which is tall and pointed inside, with a dark entrance to God knows what or where, even if Mario, playing guide, had tried to pull at my arm and get into the black, slippery place at the back of the cave, I wasn't going – all that time I'd been having the free feeling and I knew somehow it was because Cara had left the villa and I could explore as much as I liked – or even sail the seven seas – because there was really no one to stop me. OK, Cara had left a card of her show of paintings and she'd asked me to meet her at the gallery for a coffee. She didn't say how I was supposed to get to Athens. Doesn't she know that Julie could only afford to give me 50 euros to last for my whole stay? Big deal! I could hear Libs chortling when I tell her the extent of my great-aunt's hospitality – and I certainly don't intend to go.

I'm here and standing by a prickly bush that's grown right over the path, and the coastline with its bays of pale water and the deeper blue further out and the cliffs like great honeycombs are all mine, and mine forever. I can tell that Vasso and Mario feel that, too, when they haul themselves out of the cave into freedom, even if they've been up here tons of times before. Only Michaelis, without looking to right or left, trudges on as the path winds down to the next bay Vasso says is Iliodoros. He carries bait in a jar and he's anxious to get going – from up here I can almost see the flitting shadows of fish in their transparent wrapping of water, what looks like miles below.

Maybe Vasso and her brother recover more quickly than I do from the shock of being here because I'm still so intent on staring at the view that I don't notice what's happening in Iliodoros Bay, which is smaller than Marilli and without any road or sign of anything happening here for about two thousand years.

The little boat – the boat I came here in, the boat which ferried strangers last night to the side of the big caique, I'll call it the 'little' *Faleina*, is chuntering into the bay as I come down the stony, almost invisible sheep path. The engine makes a grr-rr-sound that's a bit like a motorbike revving up for a wheelie and then cutting out and starting up again. There's just one person sitting by the tiller, this time. I can see the arm and recognise it, and a lowered head which means a stiff breeze is getting up and it'll blow the smoke from his fag up into his eyes.

I stop on the path and stand stock-still. The others don't notice, and I'm a long way behind them when they reach the sand, which lies in wrinkly lines across the beach. I see them, smaller and smaller as they run to meet the little caique: Vasso waving and calling out something I can't hear, Mario brandishing a fish or a shell he's already found in this untouched, unvisited bay, Michaelis stumping along behind, swinging his jar of bait.

The little *Faleina* settles when the anchor goes down, pulling this way and that in a current you couldn't know existed in this calm and innocent-looking sea.

Stefanos stands, looking absurdly tall against the cliff, behind him now as the boat swings round. He steps up on to the prow of the boat and jumps (how does he manage it?) over the lapping waves and on to the beach.

His feet haven't got wet at all but he still looks fed up with everything and he flicks the dead fag-end on to the pebbles leading from the sand into the water.

Then he looks up at me, still high up on the path down to Iliodoros Bay, and he smiles.

What I think about this day – the day that never ought to end, it's a kind of gold colour and if I'm ill or sad I'll just hang it on the wall at the end of my bed and gaze at it until it makes me better – is that it almost did go on forever and when we finally got back to the house everything was different and we knew it could never go on being the same.

Michaelis went on the rocks near where the little caique was moving restlessly in the sea, and he strung his bait on to a piece of string or twine. He dangled it into the water that's still shallow there and of course the line got caught on a jagged piece of rock and snapped and he tried not to cry. The trouble with Michaelis is he makes you think he'd rather cry than go on wearing that funny, sour expression he often has, and his new happy look had gone.

I came down the last slope to the beach and part of me was annoyed that Stefanos had gone to help his little brother – he lifted him up and set him down in the boat and pulled out a real fishing rod (even then Michaelis looked suspicious) so his back was to me as he leant right into the boat and fixed it up. Another part of me really liked Stefanos then and I couldn't see why he shouldn't do what he does – I mean what I'd seen last night from my bedroom window. If people want somewhere safer to live – and I couldn't think what those silent, shuffling passengers had been if they weren't people looking for somewhere safe to live – then they've every right to leave a country where they're in danger of death or torture. (I know I sound like Julie when she has one of her meetings at home.) And I knew there were plenty of places like that, that dish up death and torture, near Greece, and Albania is one of them. By the time Stefanos turned round, standing up to the knees in his rolled-up jeans in the water, I know he's going to wade over towards me and say would I like to go out in the boat again, and even though I was frightened yesterday I know I'm going to say yes.

We had Michaelis with us all the way. Stefanos points out a kind of makeshift door in the furthest rock on the point by Iliodoros Bay and says this is the oven the fishermen use if it's too rough to go all the way up to Alipa and home. They cook their barbounia in here on the wood – look! – and he slows the engine and tells Michaelis we'll all be cooking his catch when we return and if Michaelis catches nothing we'll throw him back. Anyway, that's what I think he said. Then he makes the engine run fast again and we're heading out to sea.

There's bay after bay along this coast and no road that you can see leading down to them and there are rocks and seaweed in some and in another a rough wooden platform for deep-sea divers. Stefanos says (his way of speaking English, unlike Vasso's, is quite slow and kind of serious, as if everything has the same importance: you want to laugh at first but soon you find yourself listening and weighing up the words) and this is where we'll go for an octopus. But we have to go very late at night – and, as he looks at me, Michaelis shouts he has a fish on his line and we both reach to grab the rod and help him – and we knock our heads together and it's the first time he laughs out loud; I haven't seen him do it before, and I know that Stefanos must have seen me last night at the window, above the metal frame holding the vine.

He saw me there and he knows I watched him ferrying those silent men and women and children out to the *Faleina*.

And I want to ask him where he's taken them, but it's the wrong time because Michaelis is holding up his fish, which is a sort of pinkish colour and definitely small. He doesn't make too much of a fuss when Stefanos throws it back into the sea and it swims away and now I get the free feeling big-time, as if this day really needn't ever end and we could drift over the sea that goes as far as Italy and swim where we wanted, like the fish.

5

We left Vasso and Mario at work on the beach of Iliodoros Bay. It looks as if they're making a hut or a shelter of some kind and Mario is holding up bits of wood that look like planks from shipwrecks while Vasso, with her neat little fingers, ties them all together with the strong green weed that crackles and pops if you walk over it on the way down to the sea.

I don't really care about Vasso and Mario just now. I'm so pleased we've turned down the coast and not back to Cara's house that I can't help grinning like an idiot each time Stefanos, without a word (but what's new about that?) points sideways at the coastline. If I look hard where his finger is pointing, I see things I'd have missed: the tiny chapel up on a steep hill behind another bay where it looks as if no one has walked since they went up on the stony path to see the old *pappas* there – and this I see in strong pictures inside my head because Michaelis, busy threading bait on his line on the floor of the boat, says 'Pappas' in an excited voice when the chapel comes into view and makes gestures to show a long beard, which makes us both laugh. Then there's the taverna, empty and abandoned, so tiny there's only room for two or three tables, but right on the water's edge and I wish for a moment that we could pull in there, as boats must have done not so long ago. With no road down to the bay, only passing fishermen could have visited there. And I see, as Stefanos guides the little caique in towards the shore, that the front wall of the taverna has been decorated with a mural of mountains and sea and sailors in a high-prowed ship, and I wonder at the image this in turn supplies me with: of a lonely man standing down on the shore with his paints and brushes, making a fresh landscape to while away his time.

But we don't stop there. We go on down the coast and come in now to a bay that's long and a bit daunting-looking, with the sun beating down so fiercely that you can't help searching with your eyes for a tree, a bush, just anything to shield you from the glare. There are muffled booms in the distance that seem to come from far away. Why would Stefanos decide to drop anchor here? The sea is deep and a blue so dark it's almost black by the rocks. We'll all get a soaking when we have to jump off the little caique to reach the high shingle bank. And I must have shown I thought that, because Stefanos looks away from me and his I-don't-care look comes on again. And

Michaelis, beaming with unusual high spirits a moment ago, has returned to his cross, miserable expression. There must be something bad about this place, I decide. Why has Stefanos brought us here?

The fish start to bite after we've spent an age sitting in the boat (with me cowering under the little wooden shelter – I think it's called the fo'c'sle – where the oars are stowed; it's open at the back and your legs still get burned but at least your head isn't splitting). And because the real action, which I see now was all centred on little Michaelis, is invisible from where I am, I miss the first catch, only a shout of excitement from the child reaching me. Then Stefanos comes down from the brow of the boat and says, 'Sinogrado,' which must be the name of the large grey fish swinging on the line and then, before you know it, Michaelis has caught another – it's like the pink one he caught in Iliodoros Bay, only much bigger – and then there are two more.

I understand if you make your living pulling fish out of the sea, like the people who live in the village above Cara's house, it's a matter of eating or starving, depending on what you catch. But I only half-understand when Stefanos says 'dynamite' the next time one of those booms sounds right out at sea, followed by another much nearer so you think it must be in the bay with the taverna. I don't really get it till later that dynamiting of fish here is ruining the lives of fishermen and women on the coast. The illegal dynamiters are destroying both the sea and those who support their families by it. So the angry, sad mood that descended on Stefanos and Michaelis must have come from that. And the answer to why we dropped anchor here at all is because this is still the best bay for fishing, maybe because the beach shelves steeply and the rocks protect each side of the bay, like grey shoulders rising up out of the water.

—

We're in a cave that's like a shelf, a scramble up the cliff at the back of the bay. Stefanos and I, that is: a long way below the little *Faleina* sits motionless on the ultramarine of the sea and Michaelis, shielded from the sun by an old handkerchief, squats in the prow with his rod and line in a state of fierce concentration. Now Stefanos sits beside me on the dusty stone; he's on the far side of the shelf and I'm right on the edge, so if I close my eyes I see myself falling hundreds of feet down to the boulders and pebbles of the beach beneath us. Stefanos is smoking (natch) and, as there's so little wind, the sharp, bitter smell of his fag comes into my eyes and I want to tell him it hurts me but I can't. 'My mother,' I say instead, and I brush my eyes because tears are there but not from grief, they're from Stefanos's cigarette and now I don't care if he does see it. 'My mother, did she come here? Did you know her?' I say.

Stefanos shifts slightly as I speak. I realise his leg, in the salt-encrusted jeans that appear to be his sole gear (but they're not the miserable, pathetic jeans you see here on kids in cafés or by bus stops on the main road – they're OK) had been very slightly leaning against mine (in shorts; I don't want to go into that now). When he moved his leg, I wished he hadn't. But it was like the ratio of words you get if you're lucky in Stefanos's company: once he's said something, it doesn't mean he'll go on talking unless he really does have something to say.

'Yes, your mother was here,' Stefanos says. Then he falls silent again. And at first – you can imagine the jumble of feelings I'm having, trying to imagine her here, wondering for the trillionth time why Julie has no photos of my mother as a baby, feeling all this is so hard, I sway by the side of the ledge we're on and this time Stefanos does come near again, and tugs me backwards so I don't fall – at first, as I say, I think of so many questions that none come out at all. Stefanos holds his hands a short distance apart like he's measuring one of Michaelis's fish, and I realise after a bit that he's showing me the size she was when she was at the Villa Marilli: tiny, and the sad part about it is how can you tell what someone is like when they're that small?

Stefanos swings off the shelf and it's because a mini-avalanche of stones is coming down his side and a cloud of dust to go with them, and he stands – I can't think how – on the cliff, which is more of a precipice, if you ask me. I get a flash of Julie being shocked and angry if I tumble down in the swirl of falling debris, and there's no time to visualise myself being flown to hospital in Athens before the cause of the disruption appears, sliding down along with the shards and pebbles.

Oxo pauses only a moment at the entrance to the cave before succumbing to the downward movement of the surface layer of the cliff. I see his eyes imploring me to stop him, as well as a mournful, proud expression which Vasso told me was how Corfiot dogs look; they're horribly prone to accidents (two earlier dogs at Villa Marilli were run over by lorries when they escaped to the road across the groves) and even though there's a kind Englishwoman who runs a home in the north of the island for lost or abandoned dogs, they're inclined to run away and find themselves in trouble again.

I don't know why I expected Stefanos to react to his dog setting off the collapse and destruction of a mountain as someone at home would – but he certainly didn't. No affectionate laugh while reprimanding the dog – nothing – and no English-embarrassed look either, as if to say I may be cross with my pet but I'll always like it more than anyone or anyone else and don't-you-forget-it.

No, Stefanos was just plain furious. Not proud of the dog for running miles along the coast path to find its master. Not impressed at Oxo's cleverness in deciding this bay was the one chosen by Stefanos for a stay while Michaelis fished.

In fact, I hated Stefanos then. He'd hurled something that looked like a tree stump already at Oxo's retreating shape – and of course this only made things worse because the trickle of stones etc. grew faster and wider, making a kind of channel that cut me off on the ledge with Stefanos the other side and the dog slithering down on its haunches, quickly invisible.

So I did something brave. If I was expected to cower on the edge of the cliff until I was rescued, that wasn't what I had in mind at all. If Oxo was in danger, I'd go after him. I'd go down on my bum and if my shorts were torn off on the way, then I for one wouldn't mind seeing the last of them. I admit I was frightened, and the avalanche was increasing its pace, with Stefanos trying to leap across the chasm caused by Oxo to help me, as I'd known he would. After all, what would Cara say when she came back from Athens only to be told that her great-niece Alice had suffered a fall and died?

I can't say whether Oxo was pleased to see me as I shot past him (much heavier, I suppose) but Michaelis certainly was relieved, and when I reached the bottom of the cliff, he cheered from the boat where he'd been all this time with his line in the water. It's not like Michaelis to cheer, and I stopped thinking about my bruises and scratches when he did.

But all this only puts off my saying that I'm even more pissed off now with Stefanos than I was before.

He's in the boat, the little *Faleina*. He must have slid down behind the scrubby bushes on the far side of the chasm, and I can see from the shore that he's been there some time because he's holding up a tiddler caught while we were up in the cave, and he's laughing, although Michaelis can't like that much and he (Stefanos) is holding the bait jar upside down and it's empty and he's stopped laughing. And the reason I'm fed up is because Oxo is on the beach now and wagging his tail. And he plunges in and swims. It's Michaelis who helps Oxo to scramble up into the stern of the boat from the water. Stefanos doesn't look at the dog at all.

But maybe there's a reason for him having other things on his mind. He's revving the engine and pushing his little brother down on to the narrow seat and he swings fast right up to the beach so I can scramble in. Then he races the engine up again and we make a lunge out to sea, almost scraping the seabed by the shingle as we go.

We're rushing straight ahead. Under a black sky, with purple clouds that look even worse than the darkness. The storm got up so quickly we couldn't have dodged it – except I think Stefanos did see it coming or he wouldn't have got going like he did.

The first lightning zigzagged across the sky as we left the bay. If you've never been in a real storm, especially in Greece where storms come so often (or so Julie said when we had the Fight About Packing A Mac before I left) that you get used to dodging them by waiting in the groves – but DON'T STAND UNDER A TREE or you'll get struck – then you can't know what it was like that day when we struggled to get back up the coast to safety.

For one thing, day changed permanently into night. Those black and purple clouds weren't just there to signal the coming of the storm: they *were* the storm and you could swear when the occasional livid yellow streak of light appeared among them that you were actually witnessing the Wrath of the Gods.

The little *Faleina* really didn't stand a chance in the kind of seas that got up. We tumbled about, up one giant slab of water and down the next, and the poor boat heaved and sank lower in the water from all the sea we were taking in.

Michaelis had been told to stay in the shelter formed by the open-ended hatch, and he had Oxo with him, who probably thought it was more fun than being locked in the woodshed behind Cara's house.

And I bailed and bailed and bailed until my arm ached and Stefanos shouted against the storm for me to go faster and I had to lay down the oil can he'd thrown at me and rest for a whole half-minute until his yells that I MUST NOT STOP had me going again. It felt like emptying a bath with an egg-cup, but it kept us afloat – at least for a while.

There's worse to come. The lightning, writing a weird graffiti on the night clouds, seemed to want to get close to us, as we hugged the coast without going on the rocks. Stefanos literally wrestled with the tiller, but it had taken on a life of its own and kept jumping out of his hand like a badly behaved puppet. The sea was as high to one side of us as the land was on the other and the needle-sharp rocks were almost invisible in the storm, with huge frothing waves shrouding and then revealing them so fast you couldn't see where to go. But back to the lightning. It danced behind us and then overhead, and then it struck.

The wooden shelter over Michaelis and Oxo showed briefly in a peculiar bluish light and a moment later it had cracked and gone overboard, leaving a charred fragment of roof lying in the boat. How tiny and pathetic the little *Faleina* looked, without the place you could count on to hide in (or sit on, weather permitting). We were in a rowing boat, no more – and Stefanos cursed as the oars, which had been stowed there, rolled about on the floor planks and threatened to float right out to sea despite my efforts at bailing.

Then the engine cut out. Oddly enough, I wasn't frightened – as I'd been when I'd first been taken across what now seemed to have been a millpond of picture-postcard blue. I just felt if this was going to happen then it had to happen and my back was hurting so much (Julie always told me my spine was in a bad way and I MUST do her exercises, but of course I didn't) that I reckoned I'd jump in just to get out of trying to empty the *Faleina* of water. I'd like to be able to say that my first thoughts were for Michaelis – and I wouldn't forget Oxo – but I'm afraid they weren't. I didn't think of anything at all – not while Stefanos shouted at me to fit one oar into the rowlocks while he tied on the other. Not when he forced me down on to the rowing seat and yelled in Greek at me to pull, pull, pull.

I saw death coming and I didn't care either way. It's not thinking of anyone, even yourself – that's death.

We pulled and pulled and Michaelis had the oilcan and attacked the invading sea like a real sailor. As for Oxo – I thought at first he'd been washed overboard. Then I saw him tucked in the bows, soaking but okay. I just noted this, you understand, without feeling relieved or anything. The storm had taken all that away.

—

I couldn't tell you how much time passed before it was clear the sea was dropping – even if mountains of water still rose and fell all round us. It could have been twenty minutes or hours – and as neither Stefanos nor I spoke, or even exchanged looks, as we rowed and rowed, no one appeared to notice the change for quite a long time.

Then Michaelis suddenly straightened up, and turned to the prow and let out a whooping sound.

Iliodoros Bay lay just north of us. And we could see to come in because someone had made a beacon of fire on the high rocks there – and another, bigger bonfire on the beach where you could see two figures dancing about and waving.

They'd waited for us all this time, Vasso and Mario. And when the little *Faleina* came in and bumped into the stony shallow water – the sea was still rough and there was a jarring so you thought the boat might explode when it hit the seabed – they ran to meet us and we leapt out into the water and together we all pulled the stricken *Faleina* in as far up the pebbles as she would go.

Vasso was so pleased to see us that it made her quite shy. She took us along the beach to the rocks where fishermen had built an oven and she proudly showed us she'd made a fire there too, so Michaelis pulled his three fish from under the planks on the floor of the boat and we cooked them for supper. After that, we lay down in the kind of wigwam Mario and Vasso had made and we all, except for Oxo who kept thumping his tail, fell asleep. You could say that was the beginning – or the end – of the whole story. Because, as I said earlier, everything changed after that.

6

When it was just after dawn we all walked back along the coast path and left the little caique half pulled up the shingle bank as if it was stranded and just waiting for a big wave to pick it up and smash it against the rocks. But without an engine there was nothing we could do (and I say 'we', after all that bailing I feel just as responsible for the boat as Stefanos must do). We marched along in silence. As if, I thought later, we'd known there would be trouble at Villa Marilli when we got there. Otherwise, the rosy-fingered blah blah (no thanks to Miss Atkinson, who pressed a cartoon strip book of *The Odyssey* on me at the end of term and said, 'You'll be able to read this, Aly.' How insulting can you get?), as I say, was beautiful. (The last time I saw dawn was at Glastonbury last summer, but it was shit because the rain and mud were like a kind of all-over weather, the same colour as the sky.) The sea here as far as the horizon was calm and blue, a brochure heaven where a storm would never be allowed in.

There was a man standing on the terrace of the villa. It wasn't Matthias, you could tell at once – and from the way Stefanos and Vasso hung back in our descent of the last steep bit it was clear it was someone they knew but wished they didn't.

We crossed the dried-out river-bed that bisects the valley Cara's house looks out on, and paused for a minute under the shade of the great bushes – oleander? didn't Julie have these pink-and-white flowers in her hardly-ever-sat-in Fulham garden? – and from where we stood we could see the terrace, but no one there could see us. We'd been walking about an hour, and the heat was coming on already. I'd go up to the house via the olive grove, I told myself, as the sun made a bright glare on the stone steps leading upwards. I'll try to slip into the house without getting involved in whatever all this may be.

The voices came down to us. Sofia's was easy to pick out, but there was another woman's voice and it took a moment or two to realise it was the radio.

And it took a while, again, to understand that Sofia was answering questions the strange man was putting to her. '*Dhen xeroume tipota*,' she says – and I know from the phrase book Julie gave me that means we don't know anything and suddenly I go cold inside, thinking Cara must have had an accident. Then music follows the radio announcer's voice, a kind of brass band music which sounds weird here in the early morning, and when it breaks off a man with a very deep voice makes a long statement and after that the music starts up again.

Of course, Vasso and Mario and Stefanos walked right up to the terrace without thinking how angry their parents would be. They hadn't even checked to see if the strange man had gone – I could tell by the way Mario was whistling and Stefanos was just slouching along as he usually does. Oxo was the only one to look distinctly nervous, he kept trying to slink off into the bushes by the side of the steps, but Mario yoicked him back every time.

The man turns out to be the village policeman. Sofia and Matthias must have reported us missing – after all there was a great big storm last night and fishermen in the type of little caique we were in must get into trouble regularly. I can see they're looking hard at me as I come up the last flight and I can't help thinking: why is everything my fault? What has it got to do with me if their eldest son takes it into his head to come down the coast in the boat and then push on further and we get caught in a storm?

But although they're ratty as hell, as we soon discover, about our disappearing all night like that, the real point is closer to what I'd thought at first: something has happened to Cara.

The policeman sits down on the parapet and pulls Sofia's little radio nearer to him. The brass band music is still going on and it's clear he thinks it's the law that he goes on listening to the crap and he'll go to prison if he turns it off. He starts to speak, and Matthias translates. We all stand staring at him as he jabbers on and then falls silent. I remember thinking, this is a moment I'll never forget – I don't know how you recognise those times, but you do.

There has been a terrorist attack in Athens. Matthias doesn't say suicide bomber but it sounds like it – at any rate, Syndagma Square right in the centre of Athens has been pretty well destroyed and that includes a huge hotel called the Grande Bretagne. It also includes the gallery where Cara's pictures are on show.

Kiria Cara, Sofia says in a choked-sounding voice. But I see her eyes are dry and I have a funny feeling she's doing it for my benefit. Then, '*Dhen xeroume tipota*,' she and Matthias say again, as if the village policeman (his name was Spiro) had come all the way down through the groves from the village to accuse them of master-minding a plot to blow up Greece.

Because this horrible music and the breaks for an official statement by the deep-voiced guy do seem to indicate that it's not business as usual in this country today. When we all troop in to the small room behind the kitchen with the black-and-white TV we see there's no picture but the music is coming out of there as well. Spiro hangs about until he is offered an ouzo and he and Matthias sit on stools in the kitchen, looking as if they're about to have an important conversation. Sofia goes over to the washing-machine and pulls out some grey-looking sheets. And finally the policeman goes and still no one knows anything more except it's becoming clearer and clearer that Cara would have rung by now to say she was OK, if she *was* OK, natch. (Although I couldn't help thinking someone that obsessed with themselves and their art might not have bothered to ring at all.)

Then came the punishments. Matthias, a quiet sort of chap who keeps a Bible by the stove and sits in the kitchen window reading and reading it (I've only spotted him once but it's obviously a habit), grabs Mario and carries him, all of a big twelve-year-old boy, out to the log-shed at the back of the house. We all hear something hard – a stick by the sounds of it – coming down on poor Mario. Vasso tries not to cry, but tears roll down her cheeks, although she makes no noise.

I have to tell you I felt sick. If you come from a country where a tap on the knuckles can get you arrested if administered to a child as reproof for misbehaviour – or however that type of jargon goes – you become distinctly queasy when a flogging takes place. I'll tell him, I'll show him, I'll tell Julie . . . those were the so-easy things to think, but quite different when it came to enacting them. After all, what was I going to tell Matthias – and I can see him now, walking into the kitchen as if he's been up at the village church arranging the altar for this Sunday's service – was I going to threaten him with a telling-off from a sister of his employer whom he's probably completely forgotten, it's so many years since Julie came out here? And Julie herself – isn't she in Scotland with the new boyfriend by now? How would I find her? She'd left a phone number but she'd be getting married perhaps even today, and I'd be spoiling the whole occasion for her.

I never felt more like an orphan than I did on that day.

There must have been a look on my face which Matthias saw when he came in that stopped him from further beatings. Whatever it was, he obviously didn't want to go on seeing it, so he stepped into the little TV room behind the kitchen (the brass band was still blaring away from a blank set) and he and Sofia came out a few minutes later with a suitcase and a carrier bag spilling over with red grapes, the sort that grow on the frame under my window. Matthias announced they were going to Athens to find Kiria Cara.

And that was all. I could see Stefanos outside the back door on the terrace and I heard a whispered conversation (I wouldn't have understood it anyway) and then Matthias was suddenly shouting and Stefanos shouted back, and Oxo, who had been resting just out of the sun beneath the big fig tree's upper branches, slunk in with his ears flat back against his head.

I was glad to see the old couple go. I didn't realise what them leaving the villa meant then, I suppose – but I liked seeing Stefanos happy too as they trudged up the steps before setting off across the groves to the road and the bus stop. I had a feeling he'd have been in for an even worse punishing than Mario's if I hadn't been around.

Later, I found the opposite was true. But there's no way I could have known that.

—

Free – that's what we were and any talk of the free feeling is rubbish now because it means I never knew what it was like actually to BE free, twenty-four hours a day.

There were responsibilities, of course. The little caique had to be towed up to Alipa – and Stefanos and I sat in it and took turns steering if Yannis, the fisherman who was lending a hand with his own taxi-boat, went too near the rocks.

We drove to a garage in a broken-down green Fiat Stefanos said belonged to a cousin and he'd mended it for him, and we gave the engine of the little *Faleina* to the mechanic, Vangeli.

And with Vasso we went right up into the village and into the shops so dark inside you bumped into the plastic bowls and children's trikes and kitchen pots hanging in the murk from the ceiling. We sat in the part of the shop that is the Café Neion and Vasso had a lemonade and Stefanos had beer. I just wanted the Turkish coffee, as sweet as they can make it: *vari gliko* which I thought means very sweet but it means heavy sweet. We didn't pay because Vasso said we didn't need to, everyone knew Cara and the household bills would be settled just like they always were.

Looking back on that time, each day seemed to take much longer than the days before the coup (as people said it was, like the Colonels back in the 1960s but a new lot of military men this time with a mission to fight America and the UK at the same time). We didn't pay much attention to what Yannis or Yorgos said, when they came down on the footpath behind the Villa Marilli, to get their boats in the sea and fish. They always had some piece of 'news' or another, each weirder than the last, like it was common knowledge that Kiria Cara allowed the Americans to store nuclear warheads at the back of the cave by the jetty, and the path leading upwards was for spies to escape after they'd filled up the arsenal. Or that the new military had plans for here that were different from anywhere else in Greece because Kerkyra was border territory, with only a narrow channel between the island and Albania. The plans would include compulsory army service, etc. etc.

Maybe we didn't listen to any of the wild rumours because we were enjoying being free too much. I began to trust Stefanos, because although he mooched about in the olive grove under the villa with the eternal fag in his mouth and looked as if he was thinking about nothing, what he finally said or did made sense. He could keep Mario under control: since Matthias's beating, Mario had turned quite nasty himself, testing Vasso's patience by playing silly tricks and then running off to hide. Stefanos could handle situations, like when the village policeman, Spiro, came down to see us, in order – as he said – to arrange a selection of homes for us as it wasn't correct – I don't know what the word was in Greek but correct was what he said – for us to be alone together without adult supervision. And he gave what can only be described as a horrible leer at Vasso as he spoke.

Stefanos told the policeman that relatives of mine were due to arrive at the villa within the next twenty-four hours (completely untrue, but you had to admire him for it). Then he gave the man Spiro a brandy – and there was a way Stefanos said cognac that made it sound as if it was coming from the best part of Cara's cellar and not from the kitchen where Sofia kept it in case one of the fishermen needed it. And that was that. We were Free.

You'll have guessed by now that I liked Stefanos a lot and it was pretty clear he liked me. I wasn't the same as the girl with long black hair Vasso pointed out to me up in the village, who she and Stefanos's parents wanted him to get engaged to one day. The girl with long black hair always came right up to Stefanos if we were walking up the steep road to the plateia and she'd make him stand still while she tried to force-feed him with rich, creamy cakes or baklava. I never knew why he allowed this – maybe because Greek mothers run through woods and across fields with spoonfuls of food for their (male) children, and he'd simply been used to it. Either way, all that stopped after The Night in the Lime Kiln, and I can't say more about it at the moment because the surprise of what happened after that still grabs me by the throat so I can't write except higgledy-piggledy backwards.

So here we are, in dire need of surveillance, if not a prison sentence dictated by Spiro the village policeman: Mario the delinquent (his new high is stealing, now credit has dried up in the local shops because there's no sign of any of the Cara, Matthias, Sofia party returning). Mario steals eggs and honey and he tried to bring a goat down to the grove, but Vasso stopped him. Then there's under-age sex (but does it count if it's between Consenting Under-Agers?). Not to mention unpaid slaving by Vasso, who's always building fires down under the olives and pushing in potatoes (electricity was the first to be cut off for non-payment so a half-broken barbecue is all we have, or Vasso's Famous Fires).

Yet, strangely enough, nothing worried us. From time to time we put on the TV, but there was always a man in a grey suit and horn-rimmed specs sounding off, or an army colonel with lots of flags and medals and gold buttons and the rest.

We just didn't think about the future – or the past, for that matter. There were good days for fishing from the little caique – and bad ones, when the dynamiting went on and the fish hid or were slaughtered.

Every night, about an hour before it grew dark, Stefanos went after rabbits. Oxo bounded along, snuffling in the scrubby bushes and letting out yelps of excitement, and sometimes I went too because it was the nearest I would ever get to running along the tops of the mountains and feel as if I was flying.

After we'd had supper round Vasso's fire down in the grove, we swam one last time in the sea, which was red in the setting sun and warm after heating up all day. Water had been disconnected too so we all had layers of salt on our bodies – but the well below the house was a bit uncertain as no one had drawn water from it since the house was built and we didn't dare take too much of it. We didn't care.

When it was properly dark, Vasso and Mario went up to the cottage and put themselves to bed as if their mother and father were there and nothing terrible was happening in the world.

Stefanos and I walked down the grove and went in to the round ruined building that was the old lime kiln which sits just above the beach near the entrance to the cave. We stood and looked out through what had once been windows at the beach and the moon. I could tell more or less how long we'd been here without Cara or Matthias or Sofia by the size of the moon, which was swelling out sideways and really did look like a cheese, it was so gold and nearly round with a slice out.

It was in that last slice that Fate or Destiny or whatever took over, and I didn't see it coming at all.

7

I'm in the village shop and the woman there doesn't mind me standing around and goofing at the barrels of olives and the bread they bake fresh every morning, and the bacon in the freezer part, because I actually spent some of my euros there yesterday. I'm a real customer, unlike Vasso and Mario and Stefanos, although he must have hidden away a stash for his fags: sadly, they come from the kiosk and not the shop so he has no credit at all.

I've decided on two of those giant tomatoes they have out here and a slab of feta which we can cover with oil from Cara's trees in the grove and a minuscule amount of coffee because I just can't resist it. Add one of those litres of retsina that we can cool in the sea when the sun has gone down and here is tonight's supper.

At least I thought it was. I wait for an old body to have her beans and potatoes etc. parcelled up and go out the back of the shop on to the balcony there. It's one of the best shocks you can have in this incredible landscape that looks as if the gods had hurled down thunderbolts and they'd turned into mountains, with the great plain of Ropa lying hundreds of feet below you (the village is high up but I don't want to turn into a travel guide so that's enough for now), and the sea is on the other side, looking as smug and calm as a saucer of milk. The sun is bearing down on the balcony and stepping out from the darkness of the shop it's hard to see, so at first maybe that's what adds to the shock when you do open your eyes. You have to give thanks you haven't walked to the edge by mistake and plunged right down.

It's not the only shock to come today and it takes me longer to adjust to the strong light and the forty Celsius heat that comes and settles on my head and shoulders than it normally would. Dassia the shopkeeper has only said a few words to me. She has made a few gestures, too – and I stand by the fragile iron railing at the balcony's edge as if I'm asking for an attack of vertigo.

'*Mitera*,' Dassia said. And she touched her cheek and then kind of drew a line along her eyebrows as if she were sizing me up for a painting. '*Kori*,' Dassia said.

I know she means mother. And then daughter. She must have got me muddled up with someone else, I think – although I know somehow that she hasn't. After all, Dassia and her shop have been here for yonks and if she sees a likeness . . . a gliff, as that Scottish boy used to say when Julie insisted on asking him to tea and showed him the photo album with the pics of my mother about the same age as I am now. (It was the first sign of the new boyfriend from Dundee, the guy was his cousin, but I was too slow to take in the fact that a total change in my existence was about to take place at that point.)

Dassia had seen my mother in my face. But how could she have? My mother had brought me here when I was no bigger than the sinogrado fish that Stefanos especially likes to catch off the coast. Does she really remember so accurately what my mother looked like? And I know, from the photos Julie has in her album, that my mother had a special thing – beauty, you could call it – which I don't have at all. Maybe the features are similar, but that is as far as it goes.

I wish I could explain how weird a feeling it was when Dassia told me how my mother died. I knew, because Julie had told me when I was four years old, that both of my parents had been killed in a plane crash, coming in to the airport at Thessaloniki. She had described going out to Greece for the funeral and she said I was too young to go and one day we would go right to the far side of the world together and see a Sky Burial. Even then, I knew we never would.

But Dassia's certainty was somehow convincing – and then, as she went on, it became terrifying.

The shop was empty because we were almost in the 3–5 p.m. no-go area when everyone lies down in the heat. The *apogevma*, the afternoon, really only ends at five and no one goes back to the office until at least six or seven.

Why am I telling you all this? To put off facing the possibility that Dassia, half of her in the deep shade of her shop and the other half leaning round the door and out on to the balcony, was right? That my mother had been killed here – and now Dassia brings all of herself out into the giddying heat and goes to the side of the house that looks across allotments and red-roofed houses to the sea. There – in the pretty ribbon of blue that winds along the coast past Marilli Bay. Water-skiing. A speedboat – it's impossible not to understand Dassia. Then she tells me how my mother was run down and killed in the sea.

And as I push past her and into the blackness of the shop, I hear her voice insisting again and again. Words I can understand as clearly as mother and daughter – *spiti,* Villa Marilli – and I know from the way she says them and gazes at me that the olive groves and the hill covered in bright green trees and the beach and the round hole of the cliff cave should all, one day, belong to me.

Stefanos was hanging about in the grove by the Lime Kiln when I ran, or slithered, up – there had been a tropical cloudburst on my way down from the village and I'd fallen a couple of times in the mud (you can guess why).

He jerked his head up when he saw me – Stefanos never waved or used up any surplus energy on greetings or goodbyes – but I don't know what he was thinking as I often thought I did. It took me some time to realise I could read his mind in Greek because that was distinctly weird. I told Vasso and she just nodded wisely, but then Vasso was a magical creature herself and so bright she was sometimes stupid, if you see what I mean.

Now there was no sign of Vasso anywhere. The rain had stopped and every inch of the grove glistened: olives stood stock-still, freshly bathed and looking somehow grateful for the shower, and there was even a very faint bearding of green on the parched earth, the downpour had had such an immediate effect.

I crossed the dried-out river-bed that runs down the middle of the grove and then I stopped, before climbing up the bank and reaching Stefanos. Something warned me, I suppose, that a wall, invisible but as powerful as the earlier typhoon rain, had been erected between us. The question was, did I – the new, forever-altered me – or he cast this terrible spell? I could feel the awkwardness, even the revulsion that had grown unexpectedly – and God, unwanted, unwanted – between us. What had I done? Or what had he done? And the strange part is that this cruel, horrible day all came together as one, as if I would always live the past and the future of it and there was no escape at all.

I mean, what do you do if you discover your mother was murdered and no one had thought to tell you? It's like pieces of you all swimming against each other and getting muddled up so you'll never sort them out and be ordinary again. Apart from the fact that my father never got a mention from the old shop-keeper up in the village, what proof was there that Dassia was right and my mother had been hunted down and killed just out beyond the cliffs of Marilli Bay? Why should I believe her? And why is Stefanos now making a deal of shuffling off towards the steps leading up to the cottage – as if nothing were wrong between us and he'd soon be back, to wander along the beach while I swim (he never does).

And what does it do to me, to be told this unlucky place should by rights be mine? Actually, it reminds me of the witches' prophecies in *Macbeth*: Libs and I went with the school and we couldn't help laughing in their scene because one of them had forgotten to take off her head-set and her mobile phone started ringing.

I'll tell you what it does to me, it cracks me up, thinking I'm in line to run this place like Cara does. I've never told people like Matthias and Sofia to go there and fetch this, I just wouldn't know what to do and they already must know that.

What I do know is that the Villa and the bay and

everything here is tainted now with the horrible things we never thought about after Cara and Matthias and Sofia left – things like money and property and death. The Free feeling has completely gone.

—

The rain started up again and it went on for the next two days. It's depressing in a place like this, built for the sun – it drips in under the French windows on to the tiled floor of the long, vaulted room and it comes down in sheets off the roof of the verandah. The swallows have disappeared – like everyone else, it seems.

Because Stefanos is nowhere to be seen. Vasso just shakes her head and looks mysterious when I ask. Oxo has gone too – and I worry that he's escaped from the log-shed and run up through the groves to be run over on the road down to Yefira Bay. But again, Vasso says nothing.

I'm here on the beach in the funny old oilskin that was hanging up in the downstairs cloakroom, and I'm sorting shells and beach emeralds, those shards of green and aquamarine-coloured glass that get washed up after a storm. Vasso kneels beside me, disentangling the bright yellow nets that Yorgos and Yannis use when they go out fishing in their boats. The boats are drawn up right beyond the entrance to the cave and nearly as far as the Lime Kiln – but I don't want to think about the Lime Kiln because then I have to think of Stefanos and I don't want to do that at all. Something has gone very wrong here between us: but why do I have to think it's to do with me? Pure paranoia, Libs would say, if my mobile phone suddenly magically re-charged and we could talk all the time like we used to do. Cool, dude, girl meets boy, girl and boy fall in love, girl loses boy. And I hold a cowrie shell to my ear as if Libs's voice can be heard whispering there, along with the Ionian Sea.

Vasso is talking to me and she looks more serious than I've seen her before, so I understand she's going to answer my questions at last. She says Stefanos is making the big caique ready for deep-sea fishing and he's had to go up to the North-East coast to get it fitted. And if I stay here everything will be OK – '*Endaxi, endaxi*,' she says over and over – but I mustn't – '*Dhen prepi*,' again said several times – go out in the big caique if it comes in here, to Marilli Bay. Why? I ask, and she shakes her head again and then she says it's not safe to go out deep-sea fishing in this stormy weather, followed by a lot of crap that's very unlike Vasso about how the TV showed a map of the next few days (the weather channel is all that survives these days) and the sea will be rougher than I could ever imagine and the wind will be Force 8 Beaufort. You will be sick, Vasso says, but she doesn't look me in the eye. Anyhow, I'll go if Stefanos is there, I say to myself, and I promise Vasso with just the same false voice that I'll never set foot in the big *Faleina* and thank you very much for the warning.

All this doesn't bring a sighting of the caique or Stefanos. We're now in the second day of downpour and the mountains above the coast are invisible behind great blankets of mist and rain. The sea is a uniform grey, like the sea at Brighton when Julie took me there.

Cara's room is where I'm now spending most of my time. Both down under the vaulted ceiling – where I lie on the white sofa and read, or try to read, Cara's books (all on Art, natch) and in her bedroom, looking out over the sea. Just in case you wondered, I went through the old papers in the dressing-table drawer and after the first flush of pride at being able to read Greek, I had that disappointed feeling you get when you're expecting someone to turn up and they don't. These were letters of thanks – the words *sas epharistoume* kept coming up. But the middle pages were missing and what the thanks were for was impossible to tell. Sometimes I wonder what would it be like to be Cara – but it's too hard to imagine. Then I think about my mother and I wish I'd never come here. But with my non-transferable ticket and no money (the euros went on food, they were bound to because it was more fun having wine and bread and salami and things than starving while Mario tried to pull fish in off the rock), I haven't an earthly chance of getting home.

I go down to the kitchen and into the larder behind the little room with the TV. Although I know there's almost nothing left in the freezer I open the lower section and stare at the last packet of frozen New

Zealand chops (I don't eat meat) and a few packets of peas and a half-eaten choc-ice bar. In the end I take an orange from the upper part (there's nothing else there) and I peel it with my thumbnail and as I do that I hear someone come in to the TV room next door.

Then I heard footsteps shuffling out of the TV room into the kitchen and – the back door gave a squeal, the hinges haven't been oiled since Matthias left – on to the terrace outside.

Whoever it was hadn't seen me. Fishermen came and went at Villa Marilli, hoping for a coffee from Sofia or on the off chance of selling some of the morning's catch. But Yannis and Yorgos certainly knew the old couple had left for Athens a long time ago. It feels like a hundred years to me anyway: I've Lost my Virginity and Found and Lost Love in that time, apart from the fact I've spent all my euros and can't even track down a rabbit on my own.

But for some reason I'm not frightened. The view from the terrace was, as usual, that of an empty landscape, although, as Julie had joked before I left, there's no such thing as being alone in Greece. You may think you are, but there's always someone behind a tree or a rock smoking a fag or simply contemplating the mysteries of Nature. Perhaps it was the way the footsteps sounded – a tottery sound, like someone very old making an effort to walk at all. So I went into the TV room. But, apart from the pile of Mario's unwashed jeans and T-shirts, I couldn't see any trace of a recent visitor.

I picked up the dirty laundry – it comes from years of being bossed by Julie telling me I have to put my stuff in the washing-machine, she's not a servant, etc. – and it's as I'm heading out into the small area with a door to the utility room that I notice one of the garments can't be Mario's.

In fact, I recognise it. The old-fashioned type of shirt – it even has what seem to be tails hanging down at the back and the name of a posh English shop stitched inside the collar – had been in my little room, along with the period-looking jackets in the cupboard there. Its wearer must have been used to having Sofia do his laundry for him, leaving the dirty stuff, like the others did, on the bed in the TV room.

First I felt that whoever-it-was had taken my room and I was actually quite indignant.

Then the obvious truth dawned on me that I had taken his.

—

The rain has stopped at last and a sky like a nasty bruise settles over the sea. Vasso and I play a game of Connect, much too childish for either of us, of course, and when we get tired of the clack clack I try to teach her backgammon, but she says '*Tavli*' and I see the game the men play in their long hours at the taverna or in the Café Neion. It's ruined when Mario swaggers in with a fish. He wants to tease us into gambling for it with pretend money (after all, it's the only sort we have) but I can't help owning up to the fact that I was never so relieved in my life as when he pulled up his jumper and we saw the big grey fish hidden there. I'll tell you what happens when you get really hungry: you don't say, 'Mario, now where did you catch that fish?' Because you suspect he stole it. You just make a fire and cook and eat it anyway. The only thing I minded was there being no chips or ketchup.

Vasso made the fire as she always does down on the flat ground by the entrance to Cara's sunken garden. Anyone coming to Villa Marilli would think gypsies camp there, there are so many charred rings on the ground. An old well, the water has a salty taste, must have been a try for water early on in the building of the place and we sometimes wash our hands in it after pulling up the bucket (for drinking there's the cistern on the roof with a good supply of rainwater), but it gives you big lumps under your chin if you drink too much of it, Vasso says.

Mario pulls rosemary by the handful from the bushes that grow all the way down from the terrace and we sit and watch as the twigs catch and the fish's skin begins to blacken. I have to say here that there's something so still and beautiful about this part of the grove that after a while you don't even want to talk. Cara's lilies give off a smell that makes you sleepy and happy – although, if you come to think of it, there's nothing to be so happy about. We're abandoned children in the middle of a military coup which shows no sign of being a short-lived affair – and while it's true that we get news sometimes from Yannis who brings in wild rumours and newspaper 'official facts' from the village, it feels as if we're in a frozen age where the media are controlled by the army and no one will ever again know the truth.

So I ought to be sad and worried, but I'm not. Well, I am sad about Stefanos but he never comes and sits on the curved stone bench against the wall in the sunken garden and he never looks out from there on the lemon trees and lilies. He couldn't get happy if he tried. I wish I could stay here forever, by the side of the olive grove which maybe was some kind of special route for the ancient Greeks to get to the sea. Being here makes you feel you're part of something, of people who lived so long ago it's impossible to imagine.

And that is why I never asked Vasso who the old shuffling shirt-dumper from the TV room could be. I didn't want to know.

That night I didn't go back up to the house, perhaps I dreaded going into my room and finding him there. I stayed on by the embers of the fire while Vasso and Mario climbed the steps to their cottage and the black night closed in all round me. No moon, the clouds were too thick, and I remember wondering if I would even find the steps if I decided to go up to the house after all.

I must have slept, because when I woke up a greyish dawn was coming through the cypresses behind the sunken garden. But it wasn't that which woke me. A sound, a loud rushing and banging and clattering, came from above. I pulled myself up and saw I was covered in dew. I was cold. The rushing came nearer and nearer.

What I saw was a river, a fast-flowing stream that crashed down between the banks of the old river-bed and carried with it whole trunks of small trees, cans and rubbish from the village above, and as it went it gurgled and hissed and slithered and leapt almost as if it was a great big snake, swallowing Marilli grove on the way.

I just stood there staring as the light got stronger and it was possible to make out where and why this monster had come down so suddenly. It was the heavy rain of the past few days, obviously, which had made a torrent – but why was there at once so much and so little of it? – because I soon saw that, on reaching the beach, the river rushed out to sea and then vanished altogether, leaving a great stain on the pale blue water as if someone had emptied a thousand pots of tea there. It was a weird feeling, seeing a mass of water as powerful as that and then watching it disappear a few minutes later – like some kind of animated film where they think it's smart to play it backwards. But now something – or someone – caught my eye, as the flood dashed down the old course between us.

An old man – correction, a VERY old man – was visible, sitting under a big olive just across the new waterway. A bench had been built around the trunk and he sat on it quite without moving. It was the white hair I noticed, now the clouds cleared a little over the tops of the pines and something like daylight reached the grove. If he hadn't been in a sitting position you'd have thought he was dead.

But he wasn't as near as you'd think, it turned out, because I saw that there IS a bridge across the river-bed and it's just a few yards from where I'm standing, by the entrance to what Vasso says is Cara's garden. It's a wooden bridge, a bit rickety-looking, and the truth is I'd rather not cross over and risk a re-appearance from the rushing water, which would almost certainly sweep me away. And there was such a ghostly look about the old man I didn't dare anyway. If Vasso'd been with me – if I'd had my phone and there was a signal – well, that would have been another scene entirely.

All the same, I had to pretend to myself that I had the guts to go right up to the old man – he was in a coat I recognised from the cupboard in 'my' room, so he couldn't really be a spook, could he? – and I put my foot on the wooden bridge, which gave a horrible groaning sound. I paused, looking down at the stony river-bed now stuffed with empty Omo packets and ditto litres of wine and the rest, and when I looked up the sitter under the olive tree had gone.

Like the torrent, he'd disappeared. But I'd seen him – and he had looked right across that muddy, churning river and seen me.

8

The next day, or the same day if you slot in a night-time haunting (and that's what I feel now the old man's apparition must have been) as part of the ordinary daily round, was as clear and fine as the tourist brochures could hope for. I'm up in my room – yes, this is my room and I'm not letting any old ghost scare me out of it – and from the window over the frame where Cara's strawberry grapes grow red and only a bit battered by the recent storms, I can see there are even a few tourists on the beach. Others disembark from taxi boats with striped awnings and haggle a bit with the boatman. There's no sign of Yorgos or Yannis, and their boats have gone so they're probably out where the sea is really deep. A glass-bottomed boat noses its way into the bay and then a big caique, filled with people who jump down on to the jetty and begin to build a fire for their picnic by the entrance to the cave. These people are probably German or Scandinavian – they're burnt red by the sun and they have yellow or grey hair, quite different from the silent, shuffling queue of people who were on the beach a long month ago.

I don't remember how I got through that day. What comes to me is a blur of the Villa quite empty: Vasso had gone up to the village, Mario might have been around somewhere but frankly he doesn't count, if he does say anything it's usually something gross you'd rather not hear, and Oxo having gone too made the place feel lonelier still. I went sometimes down to the TV room just on the off-chance that some general or other had been shot and the military government was at an end, but natch, no such luck. Bulletins were issued from time to time with 'Information' on where we were allowed to go (no ferries to Italy, transport between the islands severely restricted) and as none of these applied to me – or so I thought then – I turned off the set again and mooched about on the terrace. Little Dassia, Athina's daughter, coming down from the village with eggs from hens that had been looked after by Sofia but were now safely in the shop's back yard, was the highlight of that day. But Dassia is too young to have news or gossip to relate, so I said goodbye and she darted up the steps to the path again.

The emptiness made me think more about Cara – and my mother, of course – and for the first time (I'd been too much involved with Stefanos before to think this) I hoped she would come back to Villa Marilli and tell me what really happened all those years ago. Only eleven years, I know, but two-thirds of my life and that's a long time to be told a pack of lies about what happened to your mother. I searched for clues, in Cara's room which felt emptier and emptier each time I went in there, and in the long, vaulted room where a desk had files and letters, but I couldn't find anything that even mentioned Julie or her daughter, my mum. It was as if they'd never existed. Sometimes I let myself believe that Dassia up in the village shop had invented the whole story, and then I felt better. But somehow I knew she hadn't made up the accident in the blue, blue sea.

It was Cara's pictures on the stairs that gave me the idea. One of them, a nerdy kind of picture of a flock of sheep on the beach and a woman with a shepherd's crook (I mean, when did you last see a sheep eating sand?), had something painted into the entrance to the cave. I nearly fell backwards down the stairs when I tried to get close up to it.

But it was there. The prow of a boat – but it wasn't a boat like the small caique, with its blunt wooden nose. It was a prow made of fibreglass or some such, modern in those days, and there was a patch of gleaming decking and a stream-lined hull with *Boston Whaler* printed in gold letters. This was a speedboat of the most expensive kind, so I'd guess anyway, and it had been kept here, at Marilli Bay. Cara must have been proud of it, or she wouldn't have painted in the name, this time of the type of boat, just as she'd done with the big *Faleina*. I felt my heart beating in a horrible out-of-synch way: was this the weapon that killed my mother? Who had been at the controls as it streaked across the bay? Where was it now?

But I could have answered that myself. The road coming down from the village is littered with fishing boats showing their skeleton rib cages, or extinct speedboats spilling out rusting machinery. The *Boston Whaler* must have ended up there years ago.

It took an age to get dark, on that everlasting day. The light went first from the olives down in the grove, then it faded on the terrace, although the brightness of the sea, calm and silvery, created a different kind of twilight. While I could still see out of doors, I went into the kitchen and made myself an omelette (Julie always insisted I learn to cook at least a little bit) and brought it out to eat by the branches of the fig-tree. I even brought a candle from Cara's vaulted room and set it by my plate on the tin table with chipped edges. And I tried to pretend it was romantic, to be sitting out here all alone, with a light that was a beacon to incoming craft.

This fantasy didn't last long, so I went indoors again and hunted for the bottle of Boutris brandy Matthias kept at the back of the kitchen cupboard. And once I'd taken a couple of slugs and was out on the terrace at my Table For One with a third, I began to feel Something Exciting really would happen tonight.

I was right, but you might say what happened was too exciting and I should have known better than to go along with the beginning of it. After all, I'd been warned, hadn't I?

Here goes: I sat on at the table and the evening grew darker and warmer (maybe it was the cognac) and I knew I wasn't going to go up to that little room ever again, with its ghost or otherwise of the old man and the bats that fly in if you open the window and the stultifying heat if you don't. I didn't want to lean out over the just-out-of-reach display of Cara's grapes to look at the beach – and I didn't want to go into Cara's room ever again either. I think that drunken supper on my own was the time I really did feel she was dead.

And it goes without saying that I never wanted to see any of her paintings again, even if someone told me they held trillions of clues about my mysterious origins. I'd had it, had it, had it with the Villa Marilli and I just wanted to go home and find Julie and forget the whole thing. (Booze can be useful that way.) I'd try Julie tonight – but of course I only had our London number (Julie won't have a mobile phone) and I knew I couldn't take it if no one answered except the BT Callminder lady telling me in her posh accent that the house in London was just as empty as it was here. So I put it off until tomorrow – a pity really, if you consider the circumstances.

I said it was dark, but after a while, a long while because the candle had nearly burned down, the moon came out. Right over the sea, huge and fat and full. It made a path right across to wherever the nearest land must be – Italy I suppose. I could fly or run along it – you can imagine my thoughts at this stage. Being so lonely felt like the best state to be in – and if Mario or Vasso had turned up I'd have been really pissed off. If you don't know how that feels, you haven't lived, believe me.

I heard their voices about two seconds after thinking all this. They weren't on the terrace, or even by the cottage – but down in the grove. You couldn't miss Mario's nearly breaking voice if you tried: he's shouting something in Greek that sounds like directions. Vasso's sweet little voice came questioningly to him and floated over the tops of the olives to where I sat.

The shuffling feet sound followed. It was less noisy than last full moon, but that was probably because sounds are magnified up on the first floor of the villa and it was from there that I'd leant out of the window and heard the march of the secret people to the beach.

The big caique came into Marilli Bay, the engines muffled and no lights showing above deck or below.

I rose from the table and stood watching as the ladder was lowered and a figure in black (it must be Stefanos) ran down it like a spider. I heard the clack of oars as Mario rowed out in the little *Faleina* to fetch him.

Then I ran. Down the hundred steps over pebbles to the sea and Stefanos and the queue of head-scarfed and coated women and men who waited there for the first shipment to the big caique.

Mario, rowing, with his passenger on the narrow ledge of the little *Faleina*, is the first to see me. He waves to me to run past the crowd and jump into the boat – and I do, only just missing a fall into the new chasm in the beach caused by the torrent as it surged into the sea.

I'm in the little *Faleina* – I'm going to get to go aboard the big *Faleina* and I've never been so happy in my life.

As the passenger in our boat leaps out on to the shingle, he lands in water and curses. The moonlight shows his face – but I know already, because he never misses when he jumps ashore, that it's not Stefanos who has come to collect the passengers standing patiently on the shore.

I'm going to find him in the big caique which sits looking enormous just a few hundred yards away. The little *Faleina* is weighed down now with more than twelve people and we're so low in the water I think the woman holding a baby who is perched in the bows will topple in and be drowned. Or the seven-year-old boy who's so fascinated by the trails of phosphorescence in the sea that he leans right over the side of the boat and tries to catch it. Or the grandma who sways dangerously, standing with the others on the uneven planks on the floor of the boat.

But we arrive safely by the foot of the ladder – and

again Mario signals to me to climb up first, as if he knows how much I want to see Stefanos and that's more important than anything else.

So I climb. My legs ache from trying to go extra fast. Below me, the woman with the baby is mounting the ladder, and behind her is another woman who presses the baby to her bosom when the mother can't make it with the child in her arms.

I see all this when I look behind me for a second, and then I push on until I'm at the top and can swing my leg over the drop down on to a deck still warm from a long day's sun.

I see Stefanos almost at once, by a tiller that dwarfs the one in the little caique: he's the captain and he looks at me as if he's never seen me before in his life. Beside him is Yorgos, and he looks at me the same way – as if I'm a piece of debris, or sea-trash, that's come on board by accident and needs to be thrown out again. The crowd of refugees comes aboard and the engines begin to race and hum. I think I hear Vasso calling my name – but surely she would have gone back with Mario to the shore? I can see him there now, dancing up and down like a monkey, relieved to have finished the evening's work. Is Vasso an important part of the family business?

The big *Faleina* picks up speed, leaving the bay after skirting the rocks. We're heading out to sea and a breeze gets up, so the passengers begin to move about on deck. Someone takes hold of my arm and points downwards in the direction of the galley and the two cabins Vasso has told me about when describing the big caique. I smile and nod and follow him down the steep flight of steps that lead below decks.

As I go, I'm pushed so I half-fall from a step, and then I'm seized from behind – by two people or more, it feels like. Then something comes down on my head and I'm gone, gone . . .

That's all I remember of what you might term my maiden voyage in the caique known as the big *Faleina*.

9

I came round on a piece of hard, flat land that was sucked at by the sea – because I could hear it, dull and monotonous and sometimes angry, so the lapping was broken by a hissing sound like an army of cats fighting it out in Julie's garden. And that's where I thought I was, for what seemed like hours, despite all the evidence to the contrary: I'd had a fall, been knocked off my bike or something, and I was lying in bed in the house off North End Road listening to the mangy cat next door as it attacked the Siamese. It wasn't just dark – which meant I'd been there for at least half a day and half a night – it was cold, too. My bones ached as if someone was trying to prise them out of me and pin them to a pirate's flag – just an example of the kind of daft idea that floated through my mind at the time.

So you can understand why I kept putting off actually getting to my feet and seeing what I could do in what was definitely an unpromising situation. I knew if I did I'd have to try and answer the questions that ached in me more than my bones, like Who Did This To Me? Do They Want Me Dead? And others which all seemed to lead back to Stefanos and were unaskable for obvious reasons. I mean, how many fifteen-year-olds go out to spend a holiday in the Med and then find a) their mother was killed in some kind of evil conspiracy, and b) they are the next target?

It can't be true, can it? If I close my eyes and stay all wrapped up in myself I can move me into another me: the one in the Lime Kiln a lifetime ago, when Stefanos spoke in Greek and I knew every word he was saying and somehow I knew why. I'd been here before, but I'd been too young to turn it into a memory. That's when I realised the past is another language and the early bits get discarded like the paintings you do at primary school, when it's just a mess of colours and sometimes the odd pebble or feather stuck on. It was because we understood each other that it's so terrible to imagine Stefanos as the one who seized me . . .

No, the only way I'd stop thinking this way was to climb out of my cocoon, the very last thing I wanted to do, and scan the horizon for a clue of where I'd been dumped. A thin yellow streak of dawn, as far from the rosy fingers Homer spouted on about as you can get, lay to the left of me if I stood looking out to sea. Did that mean we'd gone west? Not too hard to work out, we had. And, miserable, cold and coughing in my sodden jeans and soaked shirt (transparent now but who cares?), I knew I had to walk along the empty shore of this island – for standing up I can see that this IS an island and not a large one, which makes my heart sink even further. Is There Water? I say grimly, as I start my tour. Because it's what you have to ask in these situations, isn't it? And just thinking it made me thirsty as hell.

Once I'd walked for around twenty minutes I realised the true facts about the place. Above the beach – it's not high enough for a cliff – is a long, flat shelf of land which must continue to the spot where I'd regained consciousness, so the island is like a pancake resting on a saucer, you could say. I only see this when the samey feeling about the sand, and the banks of mud out in the sea before the beach slopes down to deep water, just became too much to go on looking at.

I'll go up there again. There might even be a house or, as in the village above Villa Marilli, some weird old guys who'd been nearly all their lives in America and had come back to end their lives sitting in the taverna and clicking their worry beads.

It's when I'm scrambling up the side of the pancake that I realise I've seen this island in one of Cara's paintings, her favourite to judge by the place of honour it was accorded, above the white fireplace in the vaulted room. It's such a picture of peace – pale blue sea, sand-coloured shelf and roundish rocks in the water about fifty metres out, that you feel like going out there and deciding to stay forever (or just lying on the white sofa and staring at it would do). The name, as often with her pictures, is written with a black paintbrush over a sea so translucent that you can't tell if it's air or water: Mathraki.

And I remember the place isn't peaceful at all, if you come to think of it. In the little study off the vaulted room, a tray of flint stones, carefully polished and arranged, lies on the desk Cara hardly ever uses (she'll paint but you can see she hates things like bills or legal documents). The flints are arrowheads: Vasso had proudly shown them to me and said they'd found them when they went to the island in the big caique. I told her they must be Neolithic – but Vasso knows everything like that so she didn't look impressed or surprised.

Hundreds of thousands of years ago, men killed each other on this island with the lethal flints. It's a place of violence and death. And it's where they (they? Stefanos and Vasso? I can't believe it) decided to drop me as good as dead on the lowest part of the shelf of land by the sea.

I'm spooked. Who wouldn't be? Now I'm in a prehistoric graveyard. No, there are no signs of habitation. I can't feel about the place as Cara can, loving the muted colours and all that crap. I'm for it: no water, no food, and as I stoop on the flat top of the stone pancake and pick something that looks suspiciously like a killer arrowhead from a cluster of stones in the black earth, I find myself deciding to use it if a bird, a gull or something, comes over on its way to somewhere nicer. Aly Robinson Crusoe – but I can't laugh at my own feeble jokes. There aren't any birds – and anyway, I've never heard of people eating gulls. They must be disgusting.

It's when I reach the end of the piece of flat land for the second time that I understand how desperate it all is. And how ill I am: my teeth are chattering and my throat aches and burns. As for my legs – even if I haven't walked very far in terms of miles, the scrambling up and down from the shelf has covered them with scratches and bumps and bruises. There's even blood trickling from the place on my shin where the jeans stop. So much for cropped trousers.

I'm going to die. I'm in agony and now I'm so thirsty I'd gladly kill anyone who had water, with my flint – which I've tied to a twig. There aren't many trees around here, just scrubby bushes, so that was a feat.

But there's no sign of this mythical person with water. The sun comes down on me with full force and it scorches my face while my teeth are still chomping up and down like an explorer in the Arctic.

I sink to the ground. Why did I ever get up in the first place? I try to close my eyes, but they stay wide open, as if they've forgotten I had eyelids or even lashes. Oh God, get me out of here.

Then my mobile rings. I had it, as always, in my jeans back pocket and I'd forgotten about it, not surprisingly.

There must be – in all this wilderness of water and islands and rocks and the rest – a Mast. I pull it out and stare down like a dog with an ancient piece of papyrus, at the screen. Some Greek company or other – it says *Panaton* and then flashes to *Cosmote* – comes up and then the ringing sound Beyoncé starts up again.

'Hi Aly, where are you? I'm on the train,' Libs says when I press down.

So I'm in with the Greek Gods now and their names are Cosmote and Panaton.

'Hi!' I shout back. But the signal disappears and the line goes dead again.

If you know anyone who's come back from an adventure holiday without boasting about all the dangers etc. they put up with and how great it is to be away from civilisation, let me know and I'll tell you just how unspeakably vile it is to be stuck – marooned – on a piece of flat rock where people, thousands of years ago, were so pissed off at simply being here that they killed each other with jagged stones to pass the time and there was nothing to eat and drink except rain puddles and fish washed up after a storm.

Yes, it rained here and night fell – what do you expect? At least my parents aren't paying through the nose for my horrible experience, like Caroline's at school when she went white-water rafting. But then I haven't got any parents, have I? so that's one hazard out of the way.

I'm soaked and trying not to cry and to be thankful for the little scoops of rainwater in the rock, so I won't die of thirst and that's something. But I know I *am* going to cry, it feels like the sea that swirls all round the island has built up behind my eyes, and wow, will it sting once it comes pouring out of my eyes and nose and mouth. It's like drowning without having to go into the water. And remembering Libs and her voice on the mobile – which is now as dead as one of the flints in the southern part of this horrible little isle – brings on another surge of salty despair.

Which is worse: knowing your mother was killed by hands unknown in this sea that doesn't even have tides, it's so pretty but it takes bodies without caring one bit, or thinking someone you really trusted, OK maybe you loved, maybe, knows all about that killing? AND that someone knows all about who seized me and dumped me here to die of sunstroke and starvation . . .?

No, I'll stop here. After all, if I really do suffer from too much self-pity – Julie says I do when I rightly complain about the times she stays out late, and was I ever a self-pitier when she met the Scottish hunk, as Libs and I called him – then working myself up about trifling matters like murdered mothers and attempted kidnap is really just another symptom of my malady. Sorry for myself? Oh no, not me.

I used the flint to scrape a sort of shell, a limpet I think but I've never seen one so I can't be sure, off the rock at the northern end of the island – at least I reckon it's the northern end and so nearer to the toe of Italy, but frankly how do I know? This is real survivor's stuff and although I didn't like the strong, bitter taste (I couldn't see Caroline's posh mother putting it in a bouillabaisse, for instance) it went down and then I scraped off another. I could hear myself telling Libs about it, then I realised I've become like someone back from an adventure holiday and boasting my head off. And I'm not even back and no sign of that happening. With two euros in my jeans pocket and no passport – well, I didn't know I was going to be smuggled, did I? – the chances are about a million to one against my getting home.

Wherever that may be. Villa Marilli home? Of course it's not. I haven't really got a home now, with Julie putting the house off North End Road on the market and the distinct possibility that McHunk won't smile on my moving in with them up north.

But all this brings the tidal wave again, and when the great big full moon shows up over the horizon that's got Marilli Bay in it somewhere, I gave in and started my Cry.

I forgot to mention that there must have been something not OK in those limpets because no sooner had I begun to wail and moan than I felt sick and then sicker and then up they came.

God, I am ready for you to take me now. There's really no need to wait.

Nothing happened. I went on with my Cry – but I think I must have had hallucinations because whenever I stopped to draw breath, I could hear crying sounds from somewhere out at sea. That's all I need, I told Libs in my mind, which didn't stop me starting up my sobbing again – maybe it's a mermaid, or one of those sea cows they say sailors used to think were mermaids when they'd gone crazy like I am now, stuck in the stays for weeks without a puff of wind to help them along.

Wherever the crying came from, the first thing that happened was a miracle, or that's what I thought at first: it had a dark, dripping coat and a black nose and eyes that were only just above water.

Oxo was swimming towards Mathraki and behind him was the little *Faleina*, Vasso on the seat by the tiller, and a woman with a baby sitting on the ledge. The baby was crying. That's what I'd heard.

I don't need to tell you that my first sighting of that small blue-and-white boat was the most wonderful moment I ever had in my life. A great big lump came up in my throat and swallowing felt like trying to get down a golf ball.

But then Oxo was shaking himself all over me and jumping up, while Vasso leapt out of the boat and helped the mother and baby to step down into shallow water.

'Aly, this is Milica,' Vasso said, 'and Ramazan.' And she smiled at the baby, which immediately quietened down: Vasso has that effect on children and dogs – and, come to think of it, on everyone.

I was too relieved to be able to talk to the woman called Milica. I recognised her from the big caique, where she'd been behind me on the ship's ladder, a smuggled refugee boarding the ship she believed would take her to freedom.

I couldn't even feel sorry for her, right now. Vasso had come to rescue me. She wasn't in on the plot to seize me and then dump me on the island. That's all I knew and I said it to myself again and again.

10

Here's how Vasso managed the impossible – that is, untying the little *Faleina* from the rope that attaches it to the big caique, pushing Milica and Ramazan down the ladder again and into the small boat (going down herself because the baby and mother needed help) – and grabbing provisions for the journey to the island where I'd been thrown like an unwanted piece of cargo on to the shore.

Never have feta, that white goat's cheese which Julie used to buy sometimes in the local deli but it's not the same, and olives from Marilli Bay and stale brown bread from Dassia's shop tasted so good. We're eating them as dawn breaks – this time it actually does a rosy-fingered thing and splays out its rays of rose-coloured light right across the sky – and as we eat I try to ask Vasso where the big *Faleina* with its illegal shipment has gone, and (though I don't want her to know I'm interested) when and where she expects to see her brother Stefanos again. And are we going back to the

Villa now, in the small boat? And so on. But Vasso merely shakes her head and looks solemn. She says it was dangerous to risk coming to Mathraki across the open sea in the small caique and they'd been lucky the weather had been calm. 'Not now,' Vasso says and I believe she could graduate from the School for Witches, she always knows what's going to happen before it does . . . 'Not with the storm that's coming, we'd have no chance of getting back, Aly,' Vasso says.

'So what do we do?' I say. The bottle of mineral water with the view of the mountains on the mainland, the Epirus, is already finished and there won't be any food. Vasso brought all she could in her rapid decamp from the big caique. 'I don't recommend the limpets,' I say, but somehow it doesn't make anyone laugh. 'I'm beginning to wonder how my adventure holiday will turn out,' I say, but that doesn't get any applause either. Of course, Vasso couldn't know what an adventure holiday is – and poor Milica has been trapped in a real adventure for weeks now, travelling in hitched rides in dusty lorries from northern Turkey, dodging Albanian frontier controls and the like.

So I stayed silent. Vasso said nothing. Milica's baby had dozed off at last and we had ample opportunity to watch the rosy fingers retire behind a massive storm cloud formation. A strange new night seemed to have come down over us, and a wind that felt spooky like the wind that blew at the eclipse when we all had to watch it in Julie's friend's garden in Dorset rushed at us and wrapped itself round us as we sat there, stranded on the northernmost tip of the island.

I don't want to think about what happened next, but it's the first time I've seen Vasso out of control. Well, I'll start. Whistling and shrieking, the wind had us all lying flat under a shelf of stone that's a part of the pancake structure of this 'paradise' (tourist brochure) island. Vasso is holding my hand, which is unlike her, in fact I think it's the first time, and Milica who can speak a bit of Greek but no English, asks Vasso every two minutes what the storm will do next and where can she find food for the baby. As I say, it's a rare event for Vasso to lose her cool, but she does. 'I DON'T KNOW – *DHEN XERO,*' she screams, and as Milica bursts into tears an extra big wave washes into our shelter under the ledge, bringing with it about a ton of disgusting-smelling mud. Even Oxo, who's been sleeping with one eye open, exhausted after his long swim, got up and loped to the back of the cave. Now I start screaming, too, maybe it's to show Vasso that we can all get edgy if we want to – and then I yell properly because I can see the mud is full of tiny crabs and about five of them are scuttling across my legs.

Here's where Milica shows what she's made of – and you could say it shows, too, that a mother will do anything to feed her child. She's like the pelican, sicking up a catch of fish for its young. But that reminds me of the limpets and, as I said, this storm is getting only a few minutes' more remembering from me.

Milica caught the crabs in the shawl thing she wore and before you could count to three she'd prised a box of matches from Vasso and she'd crawled to the opening of our shelter below the overhang of stone and she was collecting dried-out old twigs (no, the rain hadn't come yet and I'll tell you about that when it does) and some handfuls of ditto moss and she crawled back in again and made a fire. She threw the tiny crabs on to the flames alive – but quite honestly this was no time for ethical eating etc. as practised in Islington, or off North End Road for that matter.

Ramazan chewed away at the morsels of meat his mother extracted from ferocious-looking claws. He didn't care that her hands were bleeding or that she didn't keep any back for herself. I definitely do not want a baby EVER.

It was when the famous downpour began that Vasso seemed to change from a frightened little girl to a resolute life-saver and sailor. She leapt to her feet and said '*Y varqua*,' which of course both Milica and I understood – for hadn't we helped to tie up the little *Faleina* with Milica making a terrific knot and looping the rope round a huge stone up above the beach? Hadn't we felt pleased with ourselves, looking out at the faithful blue-and-white boat as it rode at anchor, safely secured to land?

But that was before the storm and I could tell what Vasso was thinking. As thunder had joined the sound system of water falling on the roof of our stone cave and wind whistling and banging, and as it was now pitch-dark with only a feeble flickering from Milica's fire to see by, we knew, knew, knew that Vasso must NOT go out to see if the boat was OK. But of course she did.

Milica and I looked at each other in the near-dark. We both understood without speaking that we'd be done if anything happened to the little caique. And so we kept each other's spirits up by drawing out a domino board with a twig on the sandy floor at the back of the cave where the mud hadn't penetrated, and playing with the small black and white pebbles which the island was kind enough (ha ha) to provide. The baby slept, although I'm sure he would have put an end to our frivolous pleasures if he'd been awake.

We waited and waited, and Vasso didn't come back. Every time I thought: now I WILL go, I don't care about the storm, I can't imagine how awful it would be if something happened to Vasso, Milica tugged at my shirt-sleeve and shook her head and said '*Oxi*' and I've never heard the Greek way of saying No sound so forbidding, even if it *was* said by a Kurdish woman from Turkey who's had to work for months on the island of Kerkyra before earning a passage in Stefanos's caique. And when Milica broke her own rules and rose suddenly to go to the exit from our shelter into the howling, shrieking outside world, I was the one to stop her. 'Vasso will come back,' I said in English, but we both knew this was becoming less and less likely to be true.

Can I come in? This was a voice, a kind of smooth, polished voice, and it came from a man standing just beyond our pancake lid and so buffeted by winds and rain and not seeming to mind at all, he looked like Sherlock Holmes on TV when Julie insists on watching the repeats, and I see he's carrying what looks like a box about a foot long that has red and gold squares on it, and he minds about *that* getting wet much more than himself. I'm, like, Oh how nice to see you, do come in, you knew we were giving a party? – that kind of look on my face and at the same time I'm thinking what a lousy watchdog Oxo makes, he's hardly moved at all, just lies at the back thumping his tail as if an old friend had decided to look in. On the other hand, maybe Oxo can tell whether a baddie has pitched up or not – and is seeing this posh-speaking visitor wouldn't harm a fly.

Then Ramazan, who'd make a good burglar alarm most of the time, wakes up. I wait for the scream (counting to ten generally does it) but he looks across at the stranger still standing politely there in the pelting rain and smiles at him.

That's how we got to know Peter Payne, sailor, backgammon champion and resident of the Ritz Hotel in Paris and the Grande Bretagne in Athens, when not on his yacht round the Greek islands – as he informed us once he'd come in out of the rain and settled by the remnants of the fire. You could tell he was some sort of con-man – but it didn't really matter just then, because he had news for us that we badly needed to hear whether we liked it or not. He told us the bomb blast in Syndagma Square right in the centre of Athens had wiped out half of the square although the hotel still stood. Hundreds of people had been killed. And no sooner did I try to digest this (I guessed Peter Payne knew Cara or at least who she was, but I didn't want to let out who *I* was) than this weird stranger said, 'I'm very sorry about your little caique,' and Milica must have understood because she let out a great wail and started beating her head with her hand. Obviously, the baby took the cue and the stone shelter echoed with screams and groans. I said, 'Did you see a very small girl out there?' But my voice was totally drowned out.

This was my lowest moment so far. Our visitor said he hadn't seen any small girls and he sounded as if he wouldn't have been interested if he had. Where was Vasso? And what had happened to the little *Faleina*?

The boat had been seen careering out to sea – our careful mooring must have been wrenched away from the big stone, in the storm – and then it vanished, invisible in the sea fog and huge waves.

I imagined Vasso in the little caique – washed over the side, falling through the water. I saw her as the boat juddered when lightning struck. I saw her face white and drowned, lying at the bottom of the sea.

'But I did meet the best backgammon player I've come across in all my cruising around these islands,' Peter Payne says. 'Strange-looking creature, but when he saw this' – and he opens his board as if hundreds of jewels are inside so it's quite a surprise to see only red leather and the gold and black spears the counters sit on – 'we found a place under a stone, just by the natural harbour where I put in to avoid the storm and we played. I'm not too proud to say that he won – little gnome-like fellow. I'm surprised this island still has life on it, if you want to know.' And Peter Payne laughed, while I tried in my bad Greek to explain to Milica what he was saying, and even Oxo came up and wagged his tail at the stranger and got a pat on the head in return.

So when Vasso came in looking kind of guilty – she must have known we were worried sick about her and there she'd been, playing backgammon for God's sake – we were the ones to laugh. It was obvious she was a small girl after all and not a gnome or an elf or whatever Peter Payne's imagination had furnished him with.

More important, I now knew a few things and I badly needed the time to think what to do about them. As I usually make a list when I get into a state like this, here it is:

The little *Faleina* is lost.

Cara is probably dead, killed by the bomb blast in Athens.

If so, where are Matthias and Sofia?

How are we going to get off the island?

How big is Peter Payne's yacht?

Is there room for all of us if we beg him and say we'll repay fuel costs and other expenses as soon as I get home to England (that doesn't sound true – Julie set up a bank account for me and she pays in on birthdays and Christmas and I pay in baby-sitting money etc. but I happen to know that pair of Gap jeans took me right to the limit, if not over).

Then Milica let out a sound that was more heart-wrenching than the wailing she'd done when we thought Vasso was lost at sea.

It was Ramazan. He'd gone all limp and his face was blue. It could have been the crabs – but it might be something a lot more serious.

You can all come in my yacht to Venice, our new fairy godfather says, and he shuts up the box but not without a sort of homesick look at not being able to finish a new game with Vasso. And he assures us that five thousand euros have already been won by Vasso and that'll cover all our passages to the mainland where we can find a doctor for the baby.

It had stopped raining when we trooped out from under the pancake lid of stone and followed Peter

Payne on the short journey down to the natural harbour he'd told us about and we'd never noticed, or perhaps the *Faleina* could have been saved.

The yacht looked like one of those glossy magazine features where our Royal Family are smarming up to some Greek millionaire on board his three-masted schooner. For that, as Peter Payne informed us, was what the *Cristina* was.

11

This boat is so beautiful I can't even begin to describe it. The deck is dark wood and the sails – yes, Peter Payne instructed two or three of the dozen or so hands to show us, without wasting time, just how magnificent the *Cristina* is when the wind is the only power – the sails are black! It's true. We set off like a great black swan, the storm had died down but the wind was strong and I will NEVER like anything as much as the creaking sounds of the three masts as they took their load of canvas or the slap slap against the sides of the ship as we picked up speed and went through the sea like a pat of butter.

Downstairs were cabins that were super-luxurious – you couldn't help thinking did Peter Payne earn all this with his backgammon board? but then Vasso whispered that he'd won the yacht from a Greek shipping magnate in one night at the Clermont Club in London and he'd promised a return game the next time they met. So the *Cristina* felt kind of temporary, which was even better, like a bird on the wing, so I enjoyed looking at it now. But to return to the cabins: there were very famous paintings in each of them – I even recognised a Toulouse-Lautrec I'd seen in books on Art at school and I think there was a painting by Manet of a girl standing behind a bar and wearing a stripy dress. I kept that cabin for myself, I liked the girl with her blonde fringe, but I knew somehow she was stuck there behind that bar and she couldn't have the kind of adventure I'm having now.

We reached the South of Italy in less than three hours. Vasso and the *Cristina*'s captain Peter Payne were as per usual in a game of backgammon in Vasso's cabin (even Oxo had a cabin of his own and it was when he rushed up on deck that I knew we were in sight of land) and I could see from the deck how excited everyone was already about the arrival of the *Cristina*. As our reason for coming in was to find a doctor for Ramazan, I hoped there wouldn't be too many people goggling at us as we went – but Peter Payne does seem to have a magical touch when it comes to doing what he wants when he wants to and when we came down on to the pier, where lots of other much smaller yachts were tied up, he smiled and spoke in Greek and Italian and didn't even seem to mind people pulling at his clothes as if gold was going to drip off them into their hands.

I suppose it was halfway through our visit to the

doctor that I realised Milica was looking very unhappy and embarrassed – in a different way from the way she looks when she's worrying about Ramazan. The doctor's surgery near the port was a dirty, cramped room and the cost of prescribing the baby an antibiotic can't have been high, but it soon became clear she had no money at all, and was determined not to allow Peter Payne to pay either, which was understandable, but didn't help things. For all the talk of Vasso winning five thousand euros, this was just tick, as far as I gathered, and to be taken into consideration in the backgammon sessions they were expecting to enjoy on the way up the Adriatic coast in the *Cristina*. And I, natch, was skint.

So Peter Payne paid. The baby looked more lively already, after a spoonful of the medicine, and the doctor, as he asked for our address and was told the name of the yacht, started goggling and bowing and fawning like the rest. I've sometimes thought what a relief it would be to be really rich, but now I think it would be about as uncool as you could get. You couldn't tell if people were telling the truth or not – what kind of relief is that?

Milica meanwhile was looking more and more miserable. We went out into the narrow passageway with clothes strung on each level above our heads and a strong smell of rotting food and she pulled me into a shop doorway so we could talk. Ropes of onions kept biffing me in the eye because I was so much taller than

Milica and I don't know what was in the medicine but Ramazan was cooing and gurgling like he'd never been so happy in his life.

Milica said she wants to leave us here. She'll find her way up Italy, she doesn't want anything more to do with the yacht or Peter Payne – and her big dark eyes filled with tears so I had to understand what she meant. Somehow the whole thing made me sad and that made me think of Stefanos and I realised I miss miss miss him and there's no way that will ever be untrue. So I confided in Milica just as she had in me and I won't forget us standing there under the onions, while a tiny, bent old woman kept darting to the door of the shop and trying to get us to buy.

I know, Milica says – and then we hear the hooter sound from the *Cristina* (Peter Payne and Vasso must have reached the yacht and realised they'd lost us on the way) – I know how you hide what you feel I think, she said in Greek (I can see the letters in front of my eyes even if I don't know what the words all mean: why am I dyslexic in English but not in Greek?) – I know you must think now, Aly . . . of the marriage and the times you had together . . .

There are moments when your eyes seem to have no power to decide what they see and what they don't – it's like a speeded-up film only worse because people's faces change as you stare at them, and in this case I see the old woman and Milica fused, a crone on young shoulders, and I see Peter Payne as he puffs up the cobbled alleyway with a face that has turned into a great big ripe tomato. Milica sees him too, and pulls me into the tiny, airless shop and this time I'm biffed by a plastic washing-up bowl hanging from the ceiling and I empty out my jeans pockets to show the old woman I have no money – and wow, a two-euro piece falls out and I give it to her.

The marriage? I say . . . The plastic bowl is clasped to my chest now like a shield and the old woman is trying to show me an ancient pair of yellow rubber gloves so I can hardly hear Milica's soft voice as she tells me she had work on Kerkyra with Albanians who went to the big houses and cut the grass and did odd jobs and she'd spent days scything the grass in the grove at Villa Marilli a few weeks back, and when she was up under the terrace with the big tree she'd heard Sofia talk about the wedding of Stefanos and Thekli . . .

Thekli, I say, but without any expression. I'm simply recording, and when I see that Peter Payne has charged up past the shop and turned round and is pounding down again without once looking into the shop, I feel as weirdly relieved as if I'd heard good news from Milica as well and isn't it great that a friend I made on my Greek holiday is going to get married?

Then Peter Payne came into the shop and Milica had gone. I saw a window right at the back. It was open and she must have climbed out with the baby and found her way along the next narrow street into the big city. I was about to open my mouth and shout when my arm was grabbed and Peter Payne, still the colour of a tomato and far different from the cool international backgammon player we'd first known, is shouting at me over the plastic bowl and saying, 'How dare you hide from me like this?' And 'Where is Milica?'

And because he had Vasso in his power – that's how I saw it anyway, but maybe I was doing my drama queen number and she wasn't in his power at all, just enjoying being on a millionaire's yacht and looking forward to squid in tempura or whatever for lunch – I went back quietly with Peter Payne and we boarded the *Cristina*. Soon we set sail for Venice. I told him Milica had never been in the shop with me, which should fuddle his sense of direction at least.

—

There's not much to say about sitting on a yacht in perfect weather waited on hand and foot blah blah and the reason is it's so-o BORING and there's nothing to do or think about except when are we going to get off and actually join the real world. It's different for Vasso, she's got her backgammon contest with Peter Payne, who's gone back to being a smoothie now Milica's not here any more. But even Oxo looks numb with the sameness of it all – it's like being a pile of money floating in an ocean and the only point is to land somewhere and watch people dribble with envy at all the dough you've got.

So you can see that the novelty of cruising up the Adriatic Coast wore off pretty quickly. But then, I was depressed and I kept thinking a) about Stefanos and whether he'd been in on the plot to leave me to die on the island (one positive factor: we're not on Mathraki any more) and b) about what it must be like to be Milica, trying to get to a country where people are suspicious and do all they can to stop you getting in. Not to mention the police stops on the way.

Then, obviously, I think about Thekli. Is she the one with long dark hair we used to see in the village? Did Stefanos love her all along? But none of this gets me anywhere than more Down than ever. 'OK, I'll try a Negroni,' I say to the steward, another smoothie called Alberto – and he brings me a pink drink that tastes as bitter as I feel right now. I'd take anything that would wipe out this feeling and I start remembering the rave at Libs's house when her mum and dad were away and taking E and how absolutely great great great I felt all weekend . . . But that's a long, an impossibly long, time ago. So I go back to thinking about Thekli etc. again. That's the thing with depression – it gives you a very limited choice of subjects but man, does it hammer them home once you've pressed the black button.

So I went down to see Vasso. I have to know – and this time she can't get away from me when I bring up the subject, not unless she jumps overboard, that is.

Peter Payne is sliding the backgammon counters into their places when I tap on the door of Vasso's cabin and walk in, and I must have had a pretty strange expression on my face because he blushed and shut up the red-and-gold box and scuttled out of the room as if he was a deckhand caught taking time off when he shouldn't.

'Vasso,' I say, 'we need to talk.' And Vasso, just as I had known she would, stares at the porthole in the cabin and I can see her measuring whether she can jump from it into the sea, so I was right about that. Then she puts her hands up, a sort of surrender is what it looks like and she says, 'I know, Aly . . .' in a very quiet voice. Then she begins to talk.

I'll try to sum up what Vasso told me that morning, and although it felt like a lot at the time, much of it was vague because Vasso is too clever to give away anything she doesn't want to. I could feel my heart beating very hard as if my life depended on what she told me, and if you think that's drama queen time again, please remember that I was chucked on to an uninhabited island and left to die and if it hadn't been for Vasso I'd be eaten by the gulls by now. So I have her to thank for saving my life – and that's why I can't get cross with her if she doesn't want to speak about all the things I need to hear.

Here goes. Vasso is looking smaller and paler (she doesn't go on deck ever, she's always playing backgammon down in her cabin) than she was at the time, which seems ages ago, at the Villa Marilli. She looks frail, somehow, and I try to be gentle with my questions – but they come out in a big blurt as I'd always thought they would and I see her flinch because my voice isn't quiet after all. 'WHY WAS I SEIZED AND DUMPED ON THE ISLAND WHY DID NO ONE TELL ME ABOUT STEFANOS GETTING MARRIED WHAT HAPPENED TO MY MOTHER WHY DIDN'T JULIE KNOW?'

'Listen,' Vasso says when my shouting has died down, 'you need to know that Stefanos wasn't part of the plan to . . . to leave you on Mathraki. He knew there were instructions given – but he could do nothing about it.'

Instructions? Now, at last, Anger is coming to knock Depression on the head and I welcome it, I need it, what am I doing with this crazy family anyway, Why can't I go home today, NOW?

'Who gave the instructions?' I say, and I hear my voice icy-cold and I see Vasso going back behind her uplifted arms, her eyes still on the porthole and the fantasy of escape. 'IF IT WASN'T STEFANOS WHO WAS IT?' I shout this time and when Vasso answers I feel myself go collapsed and quiet just like she is.

'Matthias,' Vasso says. 'Matthias runs the big *Faleina* when, when we take people out of Kerkyra

. . . out of Greece.'

'AND WHY DOES HE WANT ME DEAD?' I shriek, although I'm so shocked and I can't help feeling sorry for Vasso at the same time. Her own father a would-be murderer. And then I start thinking about my mother.

'Your father,' I say to Vasso and I expect her to look just a tiny bit grateful for my thinking of her when I was the one who nearly died on the island.

But Vasso just says, 'Marilli,' and then clams up.

It took hours more to get right up the coast of Italy and this time it wasn't boredom I was suffering from but real rage. How DARE Matthias keep his children like prisoners who had to do what they were told, even keeping quiet when there was a plan that involved murder? How could a man in the twenty-first century get his kids to believe they were in the Middle Ages? I remembered some of Julie's stories about what she'd heard of life in Kerkyra in the village above Villa Marilli – there was a girl called Angeliki and she'd been caught with an Italian some time in World War II and when they found out her father sat her on a brazier full of hot coals. She shows people round the monastery today, I'm told, Julie said, she's the one who hands out skirts to people wearing bikinis or shorts – and she'd said there were terrible stories about Greek village life but they all belonged to the past and nowadays girls who would have had to live in their future mother-in-law's house for two whole years before they married were free and riding scooters and earning their own money through tourism.

So how can Matthias get away with keeping his children as if it was at least fifty years ago – they have TV, don't they?

I try to think about Matthias and Sofia and I realise I've given them very little thought and now it's too late because I'll never go back to Villa Marilli or see them again. But I realise there HAD been a funny kind of tension feeling in the house when the family was together – I expect Cara was too busy painting to notice it. As if there was a secret and if the children let it out they'd be really badly punished.

Maybe the secret was my mother's death.

All of this took up my time, as you can imagine, and we were docking in Venice before I'd had time to take it all in. OK, I went on a school trip to Venice when I was thirteen and we stayed in Pensione Flora and as far as I was concerned the whole place sucks because you're meant to gobble up all the facts about the Art etc. without having time to stay for as long as you want in front of just one picture or altarpiece and that would put anyone who wants a Spiritual Experience in a bad mood. It certainly spoiled it for me.

Now I'm supposed to have a good time. Peter Payne has fixed up Vasso and me with a room in a hotel near the Piazza San Marco, I know it's because he wants to introduce Vasso to his backgammon-playing friends and he has to throw me in too. Even Oxo is allowed to sleep in our room, in a basket in the corner. But now I have the time to go and look at the beautiful things in this beautiful city, I don't want to at all.

I have to get home. I have to ask Julie what she knows about my mother and related subjects.

I don't care any more whether Stefanos is in love with (there, I've said it) Thekli or not.

It's another world and I don't belong in it.

12

I've been here for an afternoon and an evening and I've turned down Peter Payne's offer of new dresses, etc. 'for the Volpi party', whatever that may be, and Vasso, who has refused as well, is sitting with me in a little shabby piazza and eating ice-cream thanks to Signor Payne. We're not exactly friends any more after she told me about her own parents being so wicked – and she wouldn't tell me anything about this famous wedding Milica had heard being discussed on the terrace – but she's funny, Vasso, you just feel at ease with her no matter what's going on. Now she's wondering aloud if Mario is OK, he'd been sent up to Dassia's on the day when the big *Faleina* left Marilli Bay with its shipment of refugees and of course there's no way either he or his new minder could get in touch. I don't think he would like Venice, Vasso says, and she laughs as if we were having just an ordinary family chat and we weren't virtually hostages taken by a crook who would be certain to rob Vasso of her winnings after making her play backgammon all night.

We both saw Peter Payne as he came into the piazza and looked around, the red-and-gold board under his arm and a kind of lost expression on his face like I never go in run-down areas like this but I need my backgammon partner so I'll just have to go on searching.

I felt my mind being made up for me. What by, I don't know – my will, I suppose, because just as he saw us and came across the square saying, 'There You Are Girls,' and then, 'I do insist on Alice wearing a suitable dress for the Ball tonight,' I rose to my feet and ran to the furthest corner of the square and I was out of his sight. The *calle* this and *calle* that and one dusty little piazza after another swallowed me up, as I just kept running. NO MORE PETER PAYNE, NO MORE CRISTINA, I just want to get home.

They say if you walk for long enough you're bound to end up at the Bridge of Sighs and I did remember that from the school trip because Libs had stood on the bridge making loud sighing noises and Miss Tufnell got pissed off, her feet were hurting and she wanted to sit down. But even if I never got there and just died from exhaustion, I knew I never wanted to have anything more to do with Greek islands and crazy gamblers and people who try to bump you off for a reason no one is prepared to explain. I didn't want any more of Vasso's silences, either, like when I'd asked her back in the piazza where we had the ice-cream, 'How could Matthias have seized hold of me on the *Faleina* when he and his wife were in Athens?' And she'd just gone dumb again. If only I could talk to Libs . . . if only my battery wasn't dead . . . I'd be back in the sane world again.

As I ran (I hoped not in circles) I saw the shops were getting more posh and there were cafés with chairs and tables out in front of them and waiters in clean white jackets. I heard a phone ringing as I paused, out of breath, and I saw myself in a plate glass window looking like the bag lady who used to hang around the market in North End Road, filling her bags with rotten fruit and smelly old cabbages. I'd have given anything for a drink, I was so thirsty and hot – but did I look as if I was going to pay for a cappuccino? Frankly, no.

The mobile in my jeans pocket was making the ringing noise – I'd forgotten I changed the tone before going out to Greece and I flung (yes, that's the right word) myself down on a kind of plastic antique chair and heard her voice – yes, Libs's voice – coming out of it, which is, I mean, incredible! Telepathy! I'm in Venice, Libs's voice says. Then it goes dead again and this time for good.

Well, I don't know what anyone else would do but after the Terrifying Experiences I've had this was the last straw and I burst into tears. How do I know where my best friend is, in all this scary maze of streets and bridges and black canals? Maybe I was born under an unlucky star, like Julie used to tell me I was.

Then I remembered, Libs's family was rich. I'd follow the expensive shops and the malls stuffed with tiny glass animals and chocolates and gold jewellery and I'd try the most expensive hotels right on the Grand Canal. Of course it didn't occur to me, until after I'd been shown the door of the Danieli and the Gritti and the Hotel Monaco, that someone looking like me just wasn't supposed to go into places like that. If Libs was here, it was like looking for a needle in a haystack made of million-euro notes.

You could say there was one compensation. My feet in horrible London sandals were coming up in blisters and the late afternoon sun was about to boil my head, but there was the Bridge of Sighs just a few steps away. And here, as I stand now by the side of the most famous great Room in the world, is the Piazza San Marco. I couldn't help cheering up when I saw Florian's and the people sipping drinks outside, and the pigeons posing as usual for a shot in return for a handful of nuts. For a dreadful moment I thought I saw Peter Payne, but it wasn't him after all. A lot of bums cruising Venice and resorts in the Med must look like Peter Payne.

Who I *did* see – and I'm, like, I don't believe this! – is a very old man sitting in the shadiest part outside Florian's with a glass of iced coffee in front of him and a pair of binoculars swinging round his neck over a white shirt with pink/red stripes, an old-fashioned-looking type of shirt.

Yes, you've guessed. Don't ask me. I've no idea why he's here or how he got here, but it's the old man in the grove and as I stand goggling (until a Kabuki-strength number of Japanese tourists elbow me out of their video) it's obvious he has no idea I'm here. Then he swivels round in his chair and sees me. I'm frightened. A kind of chill that makes me not want to see anyone from the Villa Marilla ever again has me standing there for what seems like an age and I have to force myself to walk to the centre of the square. Who is the old man, really? Has he come after me, does he want me to die?

He waves, a pretty languid kind of wave, you might say, to someone you last saw on a Greek island – but then I catch myself. I'm a real turnip, of course this is where people meet up from whichever corner of the earth they're from. It's a matter of chance. And the old guy's decision to come here and find me – as I got nearer I could see he'd hit the bull's eye and was feeling pretty pleased with himself – was just like a million other meetings, romantic, sad or whatever, taking place in Piazza San Marco every day.

I pull out a chair at the old man's table and sit down without looking him in the eye. 'Alice,' he says, and I make a point of signalling to the waiter – I'm thirsty, after all – 'Let me tell you, listen to me.'

I'm still afraid but now I'm near him I can feel that

he does want to Tell Me All, and my Coke is sitting frosty and ruby red before me when he begins to speak. At first his voice is too quiet to hear – especially with the people shouting into mobile phones and the pigeons going up and clattering down again – but I lean right forward and I begin to hear.

The old man said, 'You know, I'm sure, Alice, that there was a bitter civil war in Greece,' and I nod because I remember vaguely the history lessons about World War II and Julie watching a series on BBC2. 'Well, the worst of it could have been avoided if our delegation to Cairo had been listened to,' the old man goes on. 'We were *andarte* – rebel leaders – and our guerrilla groups were all over the mountains of Northern Greece, blowing up bridges – most famously the Gorgapotamos – that the Germans wanted to control. We were dropped in at night, into the pine forests and we had to make our way across rough terrain for many hours a day, to achieve our results. The local population was invariably friendly – the people of Greece were behind us.'

I'm saying to myself: What Has This Got To Do With Me? What About My Mother? when the old man, with a hand as frail as a piece of tissue paper, leans right forward and grabs my arm. 'But,' he says, 'the British under Winston Churchill wanted the king to be restored to the throne of Greece when the war was over. The Greek people wanted an end to the monarchy. We – the leaders of the four *andarte* groups

– found one ally, the man who ran the SOE in Cairo, responsible for war-time sabotage of the Nazis. He invited us to meet him so we could put the point of view of the Greek people, to him and to the British Ambassador there. We left at night from an airfield at Neraida in Thessaly and we were walking across Egyptian sand six hours later.'

'Yes, I see,' I say and as politely as I can because actually Julie says the nice thing about me when I was very small was that I used to be kind to old people. I'm feeling now, though, that I wouldn't mind a plate of fries – if they have such things in Piazza San Marco.

'We were greeted very effusively by the British Ambassador and the Head of SOE Cairo and given an excellent dinner,' the old man says. 'We were to meet for discussion the next morning. But after dinner we were all arrested.'

'So the letters saying thank you that I found in Cara's drawer – were they from the *andartes*?' I say. I realise there's something hypnotic about the old man and his way of talking because I'm already imagining him at the airfield and flying over pines and seeing the Egyptian moon as it goes down over the sand dunes.

'Oh yes, they were,' he comes back to me, but not without a sharp look. 'The *andarte* were Communist and so were many of the population of Greece. Churchill's Government had us arrested and if it had not been for the Head of SOE we would have remained in prison throughout the war.'

And just as I'm thinking, oh, how did the old man get here except in the big caique? and, oh God, maybe that means Stefanos is here after all, he must see the look in my eyes because he says, 'Be patient, Alice. I have to tell you, we were two brothers, Matthias's father Andreas and myself. Our tragedy was – as with so many broken families all over our country – that Matthias's father was royalist, he wanted the king back on the throne, and I – well as I have told you, I was an *andarte*.'

'Matthias,' I say.

'Yes, Matthias,' the old man says and there is a long silence. His eyes are red and I think, He's going to Cry and I feel Sorry For Him, but I thought at the same time I want to hear more and he's right I do want to know where I come into all this.

'I married the daughter of the Head of SOE and Cara is our daughter,' the old man says. 'Now perhaps she is dead. I do not know.' And I saw he wept freely and it comes to me that old people aren't allowed to have real grief like young people and it's not really fair because if anything life often gets sadder and sadder as it goes on. 'Of course, Cara is your grandmother,' the old man says. 'She is half-English – or was . . .' and he goes back into that silence again.

Of course . . . why of course? And suddenly I don't want to work it out or try to, because I can see Julie vanishing at the end of a long dark tunnel and I don't want to lose her at all. But the old man knows my thoughts. He says, 'Julie was a close friend of Cara, and when your mother . . .'

The band is playing in the piazza and sun comes down on to the tall houses and the awnings over the restaurants and cafés and the great church which seems illuminated by a golden light. The music is trite and pompous like a concert in a park at home – and maybe because of this I break down into tears myself, lost in the entanglement that had been waiting for me at Marilli Bay, a web of loves and beliefs and hatreds that I know will never let me go.

'And Stefanos?' I say.

The old man shakes his head and pushes an envelope half-way across the table to me. 'You are returning to England and you will give this letter to the Imperial War Museum, so they understand what happened in Cairo in the summer of 1943, and how the chance of peaceful community was lost forever. You will do this, Alice. Promise me.'

I had to promise. I stood up from the table, I knew I'd be told nothing more and I knew too that old people are selfish and would rather live in their dreams of the past than enter the world of the young. Their past is another language, and I hadn't been rewarded for trying to learn it.

It seemed only a second that I stood staring down at the flagstones on the vast floor of the piazza, but when I looked up again the old man was right down the far end, walking slowly. I didn't run after him.

13

I walked down past the Doges' Palace and found a bench and sat on it to read the letter the old man had given me. But I couldn't, the first page was in French and so I struggled with the English bit on the next page and even that was hard and I never felt so dyslexic in my life, maybe because all the time I was thinking, is this why I can read in Greek better than I can in English, because I'm half-Greek and started my life in Greece and no one ever told me?

It was odd to sit in this bright, watery concourse with gondolas and loads of tourists swarming past and want want WANT to go back to the island I swore I'd never visit again. And as I read, the images crowded in: the tray of flints at the Villa Marilla, in the little study off the vaulted room – the old man must have collected them on Mathraki and given them to Cara, to his daughter . . . and then I see the sea at Marilli Bay, so much deeper blue than the lagoon here, so quiet and unfrightening until a white speedboat comes through the waveless water like a carving knife and the lone swimmer meets her death while the boat accelerates away from the bay . . .

—

The English paragraph in the faded old letter the old man had handed to me was dated Cairo 10.8.43.

'Freedom, friendship, collaboration.

Signed: National Bands of E.A.M. and E.D.E.S.

La Délégation de l'EAM est très sensible à l'honneur d'être reçu si cordialement et a senti forte la sympathie de la Grande Bretagne envers le peuple Grec en lutte contre l'ennemi commun.'

Then: *'I hope England will keep its place in progress and in social evolution and by this being able to help usefully in Greece in recovering from the terrific blows of War. As a matter of fact I am sure of it and that is why I am here,*

Signed by four delegates of E.A.M.'

The grammar of these *andarte* people may not have been perfect but when I found I could make out some of the tribute in French after all I felt proud of the old man. My great-grandfather.

'The Delegation seizes the occasion to reaffirm the pride of the Greek people in fighting at the side of the British in order to crush the enemy of humanity and civilisation and in hope that the communal effort will reinforce the friendship between the two peoples.'

The old man had explained that E.A.M. was the group from the Epirus right across the narrow channel between Kerkyra and the mainland.

I suppose it was then that I knew where I had to go.

—

First I had to pay. In the old man's envelope was a note saying, 'These were used as currency in Greece for years after the War' – and These turned out to be British sovereigns. I don't think I've ever seen one before and they were mildewy after half a century of non-use – but there were three of them and I reckoned if I could find a jeweller or a pawnbroker I'd have enough to get me home to Marilli Bay.

There were two tiny velvet bags each with a couple of ditto dirty stones in them but there was a note attached which said they were diamonds that were used to bribe villagers to help the *andarte* forces fight the enemy and Alis (sic) you can do what you want with them.

Now I begin to see. The old man didn't just come to Venice in the hope that he would find me here on my way to England, and so prove the perfect carrier for the letter from the Greek rebel leaders of the last war to British historians.

He desperately wanted to see if I was still alive. And I remembered him crying and how I'd felt embarrassed, so then I felt ashamed. I suppose that mixture of feelings just about sums up family relationships –

but I'd ask you to bear in mind that not everyone discovers their previously unknown great-grandfather in the Piazza San Marco, although stranger things must have happened there.

I know I should have gone back to find Julie – but I don't honestly think she'd have noticed if I was there or not, which isn't quite true I know, but it's *her* Wedding and even if she did bring me up she must have known that I wasn't her granddaughter but Cara's all along.

Under the lines the old man wrote about the gold coins and the stones there's a name, Spiros Pandelios, and an address in Kerkyra Town.

Perhaps the old man is trying to tell me that's where I'll find out where the most important piece of the puzzle fits in. The puzzle of my life and my mother's death.

—

It was a tourist – German I think – who was the first and only person willing to stop and listen to my question. Maybe I looked too weird (I've done something about that, I'll tell you later) and people thought I was bonkers or a thief, because my question was, how can I find a second-hand jeweller and how would I get there? And no one knew the answer except, as I say, this one guy who started showing me maps and things and even went so far as to open a guide book and a pocket dictionary, so I was the one who thought she'd stumbled across an obsessive-compulsive-disorder type, i.e. a weirdo.

Still, what would I have done without him? By the time I realised I'd never shake him off we'd reached the little street with Missoni and round the corner Harry's Bar and a lot of celebs were pushing past me and my helper with disgusted Venice-in-summer-is-impossible faces – if they'd had lace handkerchiefs they'd have held them over their noses. We will take the *motoscafo*, says Johann or Hans (I never found out his name), and he kind of pushed me along the outside of the Hotel Monaco – I recognised it from when I'd been looking for Libs – and we went down two more streets and turned left again and sure enough we were back at the Grand Canal and there's a bus stop and even a waterbus sitting at it, as if this was a film and it had all been set up beforehand.

It is Zattere, said the German guy. This is where we go.

But then something caught my eye. There were few people on this particular quay – just a few Moroccans darting about with fake Gucci handbags tied together with string and what looked like two gypsy women (but I knew better by now, like Milica they were probably not gypsies at all but illegal immigrants desperately trying to escape torture and starvation in their own country) and the two women were leading a great pack of dogs, also tied with string as if they were for sale, like the handbags or the fake furs draped on steps and in doorways.

Wait a minute, I said, and honestly I nearly fell into the Grand Canal just then because the bus platform is not the place to change your mind about your journey if you're going by *motoscafo*. And I shouted – and even the German guy looked as if he was about to run away from me or disown me, like people do if they're caught with a criminal – and as I shouted all the dogs burst into an enormous barking and this time people did rush out from shuttered shops and houses to see what all the commotion was about.

What I'd shouted was 'OXO!' and of course that meant nothing to anybody except poor Oxo himself. His string lead was all muddled up with the others and it was terrible seeing him struggle to get to me while all the time he was pulled along by the women who were running now because they feared they'd be reported by the residents and sent to prison. All the thoughts that raced through my head were, like, Oxo, how did Vasso let you go? – and then, God, does that mean Vasso isn't OK? I should have gone back to the hotel and told her everything the old man had said to me in the square – and then there I was running myself but with no idea of where or how I'd get out of this place where the bridges and shuttered buildings were all part of a jigsaw puzzle I could never do.

Seeing me run in all directions made the women

scream and they fell back as if I was a terrorist who was out to kill them, and all the dogs came crowding right to the edge of the water and even the *motoscafo* driver stopped the engine and sat staring at us. But I saw this is just Venice where things blow up and then they disappear again, as if water's closed over the violence or the parties or whatever as if they never happened at all.

The dogs all slunk away, and I was left with Oxo. A cheer went up from the Venetians waiting in the bus. They'd seen the show and it was time to go on. The German guy had vanished and, I forgot to say, what was so great about all those people on the boat was they paid my fare to Zattere, wherever that is, and they added in a euro or two for Oxo too.

—

I was quite serious when I said I should have gone to tell Vasso everything I'd been told today, and I should probably have insisted that she came with me and found a way back to the island – but I didn't really want to. There are facts I need to unravel for myself before I confide them to anyone. Suppose Stefanos is part of the plot to kill my mother and then myself (you heard me say it), for after all I can't have been expected to survive on Mathraki. Suppose Vasso told him who I am . . . and worst of all suppose Matthias is back at Marilli Bay and waiting for me when I get there.

So I've just dodged the first big responsibility I've been landed with in my life. I've left the child who saved my life to fend for herself in a corrupt city, with a ditto corrupt minder, Peter Payne, who'll exploit her and then rob her. How could I have done this? But I did. After all, my life had been threatened and Vasso's hadn't – nor is it likely to be.

It doesn't sound good, does it?

—

Zattere turns out to be on the opposite side of Venice to the posh hotels and Piazza San Marco and if I had to live here, this is where I'd choose. It's kind of run-down and shabby and people like to tell you how to find the way to a second-hand jeweller instead of hurrying away from you. So I changed my sovereigns and two of the little velvet bags of uncut diamonds into enough money to take me by train down to Brindisi which is the port across the Ionian Sea from Kerkyra. And I even found a second-hand clothes shop as well, a kind of Venetian Oxfam, and kitted myself out in Italian vintage.

14

I'm on the train – that's me talking to Libs after I texted her and said, you'll never guess, I'm just leaving Venice now, you dickhead, where've you been? And it's great to imagine her saying her mum and dad can't decide whether to take a trip to the Greek islands, or would it be too hot at this time of year? And greater still to be able to say that's where I'm going, with my dog, of course, and she screams and says WHAT DOG? So I'm a few points up on that one.

I won't go into the utter hell-hole of Brindisi, especially after a long train journey all the way down Italy, looking out at the funny towns like Bari and the bright blue sea which made me long to be back at Marilli Bay more than ever. I'll pass over the ferry, there were no cabins left and I had to sit in the bar all night with a whole lot of Italian men of about eighteen who kept pointing and whistling, which never happens in Greece. Maybe the Italian men are all mother-fixation victims because they're Catholic and pray to the Virgin

Mary, that's what Gill at school said before I left for my summer holiday and she told me I was lucky to be going to Greece and not to Italy. Whatever.

Of course, when the ferry reached the port at Kerkyra, I was fast asleep on two bright orange plastic chairs and the blokes were all being quiet so as not to wake me and that about puts an end to stereotypes.

The port was just as lovely and homey as I'd imagined. Homey because there were at least fifty big caiques, all like the *Faleina* but not as beautiful, obviously, and instead of remembering how awful it had been when I was seized etc. I just knew I Must Must Must go aboard ours again and this time be happy. What a hope! Yet it got me through the customs and explaining I'd lost my passport. When I gave Villa Marilli as the address I was going to, they'd shrugged as if there weren't armed police standing all round and clearly no change in the military regime since I'd been dumped in Mathraki, and they made me sign a form and waved me through.

It's very early morning, an hour earlier than Italian time and I'm desperate for breakfast, but it's peculiar in Greece, you have to eat different things in different places, like your morning yoghurt is only found in a dairy, your coffee (only Turkish here at the port) in a Café Neion and bread at a baker's shop. None of these has ever tasted so good even if it was a business getting them – and I even found a cab, waiting for ferry passengers and not too grumpy at a) taking a dog or

b) the short distance Mr Spiros Pandelios's office turned out to be. Now I'm sitting in his office after a lady with a beehive hair-do – she looks like an actress in one of the *Carry On* films Julie's boyfriend likes to watch on TV Gold (you can see why I hate him) – has said my name into a telephone and I'm finally admitted.

Spiros Pandelios is the lawyer who deals with all of Cara's family business and he says he considers himself a family member, which I find definitely daunting. Do I tell him what the old man said to me? What if the old man is some kind of made-up person, a con-man like Peter Payne? I don't know what to do, so I just keep my mouth shut. But Mr Pandelios, who is about fifty and good-looking in a sort of old-fashioned way, regular features and very black hair etc., smiles at me and asks Beehive for two coffees and he says, 'This is Alissa,' that's how he pronounced it anyway, 'And she's come today to talk about the Marilli Bay estate.'

All this sounds very grand, so I lower my eyes while Beehive simpers at me. Once she's fetched in the hot, strong Metriou coffee in thick white china cups, Pandelios begins.

'Alissa, you need to know the story behind Marilli Bay and I fear you may find it farcical,' the lawyer says.

Farcical? I just kept silent, as usual.

'Your great-grandfather Andreas, as I believe you must know by now, was an *andarte*, a rebel leader, in the last war.' I nod at this. If he knows I know, why is he telling me?

But lawyers can't help themselves I suppose and on he goes: 'There were two brothers, Andreas and Yannis,' he says.

Yes yes, I want to get to Matthias and Stefanos, I'm thinking, but I look polite as if all this is news to me. The two brothers unfortunately fell in love with the same woman, Pandelios says. She was the daughter of a distinguished Englishman and her name was Irene. Well, the brothers came to an understanding after both had proposed and Irene had turned them both down – she liked Andreas, you see, and she waited for them to work something out between them.

I'm getting that don't give me any more of the past feeling, but I nod my head politely again.

'So Andreas arranged with Yannis that he would take the lady and his brother would have the land at Marilli Bay. This worked quite well for Yannis as he had the revenue from the vines and olives. Irene's English money built the villa and she and Andreas had a daughter, Cara. Although Yannis was a royalist in the dreadful years of the Civil War and Andreas was a republican, they got on well enough – until Yannis's son Matthias . . .'

'Oh,' I say, and this time it's the lawyer who nods his head at me.

'Yannis had married a village woman, Thekli by name, who was Matthias's mother. It is possible that her determination and that of her family in the village to gain control of all of Marilli Bay led to Matthias's actions once Yannis died.'

So this was it, I thought, and I felt a kind of grey miserable wave come across me and at that moment Oxo slunk into the office and I stroked and stroked him, I've never been so glad to see anything in my life. 'Matthias killed my mother,' I said across the desk to Spiros Pandelios.

'Alissa *mou*, this cannot be proved, but it is certain that Matthias wanted the house as well as the land. When you came out here as a child with your mother – '

'Did I? Did I?' I hear myself babbling like a fool.

'You were very small,' Pandelios says and sighs. 'After your mother's . . . accident . . . Kiria Cara did not feel able to take on the responsibility of bringing you up and a friend of your mother's who had come out for a visit, her name was . . .'

'Julie,' I say.

'*Ne*, Despinis Yoolie,' says the lawyer. 'You are given to her . . .'

'I know the rest,' I say. 'It was obvious that the arrival of a new heir to the villa would stir things up,' I say. 'So Matthias has his children do whatever he tells them?' I go on, hoping it sounds a casual question. Would Stefanos have known what Matthias . . . planned to do with me?

'I have heard from Andreas, God bless his many

years,' the lawyer replies. 'I have heard of you going on the big *Faleina* and I believe you were instructed not to by Andreas and by little Vasso . . .'

'Instructed!' I say and I know I'm angry, really angry. 'It's my fault for going on the caique,' I said, 'that's bound to get me knocked off, is it? What are all these instructions in this family? Matthias tells his son Stefanos and it's all fixed up . . .'

'Alissa, I must tell you that Stefanos is not Matthias's son,' Pandelios breaks in. 'Matthias had no children, but as his family grew richer and more powerful in their village and in surrounding communities, they took over children of their clan who had been orphaned.'

All this time, I was feeling sicker and sicker, I knew this little cramped room with its files stacked up to the ceiling and a view of the stone wall of the next-door building would very likely contain a secret I did not, repeat did NOT, want to hear. 'You're going to tell me Stefanos is my brother or something,' I said in an attempt to keep my tone light and making-small-talk-like.

'No, no.' Pandelios laughs as if he'd joined in the we're-all-at-a-cocktail-party game. 'But he is the real brother of Vasso, and Matthias threatened him that if he didn't obey instructions, he would do harm to Vasso.'

This time I stayed silent because there really was nothing to say.

'We will go to Villa Marilli together,' Spiros Pandelios says. 'It has occurred to me, Alissa, that you may be able to assist me in bringing the wicked Matthias to justice – if you don't object to a little danger, that is.'

That was how we all drove across the island in Pandelios's Hyundai car – that is, the lawyer and Beehive, who must have been some sort of girlfriend, and Oxo snuffling with excitement as we got closer and closer to the sea.

15

I might never have left. The road as it comes down past the village and the stopping-place where you have to get out and then walk down through the groves and the sight of the roof of the house the first time when you're at a bend under the tall cypress there were so familiar to me. I came here when I was too young to remember, and I'm here again now. There seems little more than a sort of wavy line like a morse code message I've forgotten how to decipher between the two times.

Of course, everything's different now. We have to walk because there's no little caique to meet us at Alipa. And who would there be to bring it over – if it hadn't been blown out to sea at Mathraki? Stefanos must believe I accuse him of attempted murder and he wouldn't come. Cara is long gone.

Yet, as I ran ahead of the lawyer and his girlfriend, and with Oxo bounding the fastest down over ruined terraces and through the citrus plantations the locals keep fenced (but there's always a hole in the gate for Oxo and he knows each one of them), I realise there is life going on at Villa Marilli after all.

There's music, loud Greek music, bouzouki and wailing voices singing the songs of celebration, joy, melancholy all mixed up together in one terrible song. I know what it is, we've heard it down from the village most Saturdays, and I stop just above the house and although it's sunny and hot my teeth are chattering.

It's a wedding party – Stefanos's wedding, Spiros Pandelios says from just behind me. And I know without asking that Thekli is the bride, although the lawyer, not noticing what I'm feeling inside, says, 'There's No Time to Waste, Alissa. He marries a cousin, her name is Thekli, it is arranged by Matthias in order to strengthen their claim to the whole estate.' And he takes my hand and forces me to go more slowly and with some kind of dignity to the top of the 86 pebble-laid steps that go down to the terrace and the big fig tree that stands over it from the *stoa* below. We could simply be wedding guests, come to celebrate the dynastic union of a pair of cousins with roots in Marilli Bay.

When we're half-way down the steps and can see on to the terrace, I stop, and Oxo, who's already been down there, comes rushing up with a hunk of meat in his mouth and streaks of some kind of creamy sauce all down his coat. As I call out to him to stand still while I dab with a tissue the Girlfriend passes down the steps to me, the assembled guests look up from the terrace and the music stops and we all freeze, as if we are known to be bad fairies who will bring misfortune instead of the other way round, with Matthias the evil-doer and both myself and Stefanos innocent of anything other than having been, being still – well, I won't say it now.

Then there he is, looking miserable in a pathetic suit with a wilting carnation in his buttonhole and nothing on earth can stop me from racing down to be with him. I understand, I want to say, I know why you went cold, trying to warn me that I was going to be killed . . . I know now, I'm sorry, sorry, sorry I thought badly of you.

But it's too late. The lawyer catches me as I stumble past the dog and the music starts up again so he has to pull me right up close to make himself heard. He tells me what I must do. I only realise I'm holding a gun, a fancy-looking thing like a water-pistol, when he turns to walk away. And before he goes he pulls a great wad of euro notes from his pocket and presses them into my hand.

So, once I've tucked the gun away in the top of my jeans, nothing to arouse suspicion yet. People come with money to give the bride and groom at weddings – that's what I am, as far as they're concerned, an English well-wisher, a distant relative of Kiria Cara who is no longer here.

I obey Pandelios's instructions and run down the

back steps under the olives to the beach. 'Find Yorgos, offer him the money,' says Pandelios in my ear as I run, 'Return the way you came and I'll meet you outside Matthias's cottage. Quick! Now!'

Yorgos was inside the cave, cleaning out his boat before going up to join in the festivities. He's a bit thick but a friendly type, and when he sees Oxo he lets out a welcoming shout. 'Yorgos,' I say, running into the dark cave which smells of pee in summer because the tourists use it as if it had been formed by Nature for their convenience, 'Yorgos, look, I have this for you.' And I wave the wad of notes at him as Pandelios had told me to do.

Yorgos backs away from me and as he does so I see something rusty nearly trip him up beyond his little fishing-boat at the back of the cave. A wheel – yes, a steering-wheel, and I think of Cara's picture and the nose of the speedboat, the *Boston Whaler*, white and gleaming in her picture in the vaulted room.

'*Oxi*,' Yorgos says, as I pursue him with the money. '*Dhen thelo* – I don't want it – '

And I say, 'But, Yorgos, Matthias wants me to give this to you.'

Now the fisherman looks baffled, but trying to be cunning too, because he senses a trick here and the Greeks are better at tricks than anyone else in the world.

'He miscounted the first time,' I say. 'How much was it again?'

The entrance to the cave grows suddenly dark and Matthias is there. My throat goes dry and my heart beats as if it wants to jump out of my body. For God's sake, Mr Pandelios, how have you let this happen? Help me! I'm crying out – but only to myself, you understand, because there's Anger growing in me, this time as huge as a monster, and it's directed at Matthias, not the poor man who drove the white speedboat and ran my mother down. 'How much was it?' I say, as the gun jumps out into my hand and two paces later I'm across the wet sand and pointing it at Matthias's throat.

'Five thousand euros,' Yorgos says, so quiet his words are almost drowned out by the sea. He's too frightened now to move, while Matthias stands as if he's been frozen to stone by the entrance to the cave.

'Dead or alive?' I say, and Yorgos begins to blubber and muddle up his words, saying it was drachmas, then it was so long ago, and I know he must mean he was paid in the old currency to murder my mother and I wave the gun away from Matthias and go for Yorgos and just as Matthias leaps at me the shadows of two people fall across the floor of the cave and Spiros Pandelios and the blonde woman walk in and Matthias pushes past them and runs . . .

—

The police were all over Marilli Bay and the villa, by the time I walked up there with a sobbing Yorgos.

Pandelios had gone after Matthias and he'd been caught on the first landing of the back steps under the olives on the way up to the house. A bright blue agapanthus lay trampled on the flagstones. But, apart from this, there is no sign of the fight he must have put up when they came down and seized him in mid-flight.

They took Yorgos next, but really only because the fisherman begged them to. He'd been told to give the woman swimming out in the bay all those years ago a fright – just for fun – that's what Matthias had told him to do, he said, and the half-wit had taken money to do it. The trouble was, a freak wave came and threw him up nearer than he was meant to go to the swimmer . . .

I don't want to think about it. Yorgos is a fool but obviously he can't answer the question, now I know how much you were paid to kill me, how much did they give you to keep me alive, because dumping me on the island of Mathraki would leave Nature to work that one out for herself.

—

There's nothing like a police presence to spoil the atmosphere at a party – I remember Julie saying that when she went to a book group and left her handbag out in the street and the police were called, in case. She was right, though – the wedding party simply fizzled out and what must have been the bride's immediate family straggled up the steps to the groves and then the road back up to the village.

So here's the Miracle, and it's been a long time coming.

I'm standing on the edge of the sea and watching the bright ladder the sun makes across the water and wishing I could climb it and disappear just where the sea and sky meet, when I see something coming up from the south and making its way in to Marilli Bay.

And as it grows nearer I see it's the little *Faleina* – and it was a Miracle because Stefanos, who'd seen it from the terrace and run along the cliff and down to Iliodorus Bay to jump in, said the little caique had definitely been headed for home after being lost all that time ago in the storm at Mathraki.

The boat came in gently and bumped against the jetty – I think it was the only clumsy mooring Stefanos ever made in the little *Faleina*.

But then I didn't really blame him – there'd been plenty to take his mind off where he was going, and the sun was in his eyes, anyway.

The main thing is, the little *Faleina* has come home. And so have we.

epilogue

The end of summer has come. If you stand on the terrace the ladder the sun makes across the sea has shifted away from Italy to point directly up the olive grove, burnishing the silver-grey leaves and falling right into the sunken garden where I sit doing my homework for next term's exams.

Julie brought out the papers – and when she goes back she'll take the letter to the Imperial War Museum with her, though whether it will change the historians' view of the Civil War in Greece it wouldn't be easy to say. The old man is happy, at least: Matthias awaits trial for inciting the fisherman Yorgos to run down my mother in the sea all those years ago. And the old man has his room back, he's glad of that, too.

It's hard for me to think about Cara, who, we finally heard, had been killed in that first Athens bomb blast. Somehow she's stuck in my mind as a grandmother I only knew for a few hours and talking to Julie about her is all I have.

Where am I? In the cottage below the Villa Marilli, with Stefanos. The big fig tree stands between us and the terrace, and for weeks now we've been pulling the fruit from the branches and eating and eating and eating, as if this feast will eradicate forever the betrothal party I came down to find when I returned here with the lawyer and his girlfriend.

We're happy, and if I didn't miss Vasso so much everything here would be perfect. We hear from her from time to time: she's in America, or the Caribbean, winning backgammon championships, and now chess. She doesn't mention Peter Payne, so he must have disappeared from the scene.

Sometimes, when the gold ladder is right down and I'm basking on the last rungs in the garden, Julie comes and we sit together in silence. Then I ask her about my mother, and she says after my mother was killed Cara just couldn't cope with looking after a grandchild, and Julie had been happy to look after me. My father, she tells me, really did lose his life in the Thessaloniki plane crash on his way to join my mother at Marilli Bay. He would have been too late, of course.

That's all.

the end

Also by EMMA TENNANT from WWW.MAIAPRESS.COM

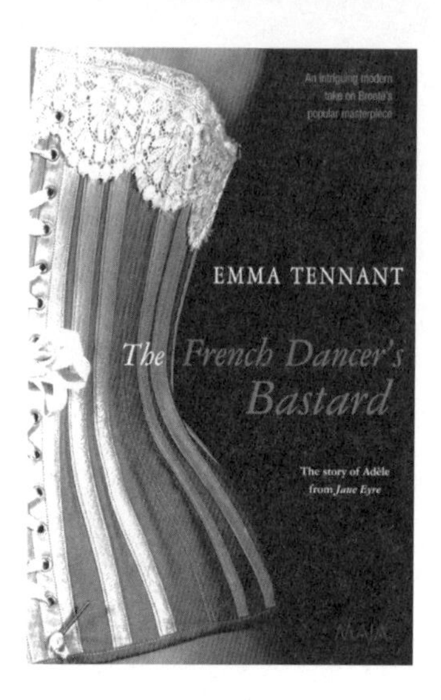

THE FRENCH DANCER'S BASTARD

£8.99 ISBN 978 1 904559 23 8

Adèle Varens is only eight when she arrives at Thornfield Hall to live with the forbidding Mr Rochester, a man who may or may not be her father. She longs to return to the glitter of Paris and to the mother who has been lost to her. Her loneliness would be complete were it not for Jane Eyre, the young governess who arrives to care for her, although Adèle at first regards her with suspicion and dislike.

But there is another shadow hanging over their lives: the dark secret locked away in a high garret. Adèle's curiosity will imperil them all, shatter their happiness and finally send her fleeing, frightened and alone, back to Paris.

'It is heartening to read a narrative which has the courage to take us from myth to fairy tale . . . Charlotte Brontë would have been proud' Michelene Wandor, *TLS*

'A delight to read . . . an enjoyable twist on a classic tale' *Big Issue*

'A zig-zagging drama . . . enjoy the breathless twists and turns' *Guardian*

Also by EMMA TENNANT from WWW.MAIAPRESS.COM

THE HARP LESSON

£8.99 ISBN 978 1 904559 16 0

Set in the years around the French Revolution, this atmospheric and poignant novel explores the life of Pamela Sims, La Belle Pamela. At a young age she is taken from a humble home in England to the French court, where she is brought up in luxury as the illegitimate daughter of the beautiful Madame de Genlis and the Duc d'Orléans.

Recounted through the voices of Pamela and her daughter, this novel describes how the past has shaped their extraordinary lives, capturing the atmosphere of eighteenth-century France and the complexity of a world where your origins create your identity.

'A vivid portrait of the times' ***The Times***

'A wonderfully readable narrative of seductive, visual dreaminess' ***TLS***

'The romance of Pamela's story is irresistible' ***Independent on Sunday***

'Eighteenth-century private life through the eyes of a mysterious beauty . . . riveting' Antonia Fraser

PEMBERLEY REVISITED

£8.99 ISBN 978 1 904559 17 7

Elizabeth wins Darcy, and Jane wins Bingley – but do they 'live happily ever after'? These bestselling sequels to *Pride and Prejudice* ingeniously pick up threads from Jane Austen's timeless novel, in a lighthearted and affectionate look at the possible subsequent lives of the main characters. *Pemberley* tells of Elizabeth's difficulty in producing a son and heir; while *An Unequal Marriage* continues the story of the Bennets and their wider circle into the next generation.

'Tennant has an ear for Jane Austen and mimics her dialogue perfectly' ***Sunday Business Post***

'Tennant's narrative is made compelling by her utter mastery of Austen's style' ***The New York Times***

'Delicious sequels' ***Publishing News***

Also available from WWW.MAIAPRESS.COM

Merete Morken Andersen AGNES & MOLLY

£9.99 ISBN 978 1 904559 28 3

The story of two friends and the man they both desire. When he asks Molly to take care of his two children, Agnes is jealous. She comes to help, and a real struggle for power begins, with the women battling for the affections of the children. A richly atmospheric novel about friendship, jealousy and love.

Merete Morken Andersen OCEANS OF TIME

£8.99 ISBN 1 904559 11 5 | 978 1 904559 11 5

A divorced couple confront a family tragedy in the white night of a Norwegian summer. International book of the year (*TLS*), longlisted for The Independent Foreign Fiction Prize 2005 and nominated for the IMPAC Award 2006.

Michael Arditti GOOD CLEAN FUN

£8.99 ISBN 1 904559 08 5 | 978 1 904559 08 5

A dazzling collection of stories provides a witty yet compassionate and uncompromising look at love and loss, desire and defiance, in the 21st century.

Michael Arditti A SEA CHANGE

£8.99 ISBN 1 904559 21 2 | 978 1 904559 21 4

A mesmerising journey through history, a tale of dreams, betrayal, courage and romance told through the memories of a fifteen-year-old. Based on the true story of the Jewish refugees on the SS *St Louis*, who were forced to criss-cross the ocean in search of asylum in 1939.

Michael Arditti UNITY

£8.99 ISBN 1 904559 12 3 | 978 1 904559 12 2

A film on the relationship between Unity Mitford and Hitler gets under way during the 1970s Red Army Faction terror campaign in Germany in this complex, groundbreaking novel. Shortlisted for the Wingate Prize 2006.

Booktrust London Short Story Competition UNDERWORDS: THE HIDDEN CITY

£9.99 ISBN 1 904559 14 X | 978 1 904559 14 6

Prize-winning new writing on the theme of Hidden London, along with stories from Diran Adebayo, Nicola Barker, Romesh Gunesekera, Sarah Hall, Hanif Kureishi, Andrea Levy, Patrick Neate and Alex Wheatle.